THE SEVEN DEADLY SINS

Rachel Billington, Michael Carson,
William Douglas Home,
Andrew Greeley, H. R. F. Keating,
Kate Saunders, Morris West

Illustrations by Clara Vulliamy
Introduction by Peter Stanford

British Library Cataloguing in Publication Data
The seven deadly sins.
1. Fiction in English, 1945– – Anthologies
I. Greeley, Andrew M. (Andrew Moran) *1928–*
823.91408

ISBN 0-340-54154-7
ISBN 0-340-53854-6

*Printed in Great Britain for Hodder and Stoughton Limited, Mill Road,
Dunton Green, Sevenoaks, Kent by Clays Limited, St Ives plc. Photoset by
Rowland Phototypesetting Limited, Bury St Edmunds, Suffolk.*

*Hodder and Stoughton Editorial Office: 47 Bedford Square, London
WC1B 3DP.*

Contents

Acknowledgments

A Time for Tea © 1990 *Rachel Billington*
Return to Sender © 1990 *Michael Carson*
Perchance to Dream © 1990 *William Douglas Home*
Pride Before a Fall © 1990 *Andrew Greeley*
Death Hath Also This © 1990 *H. R. F. Keating*
She Went of Her Own Accord © 1990 *Kate Saunders*
Take Heed! © 1990 *Morris West*

These stories were first published in the *Catholic Herald* during Lent 1990.

THE SEVEN DEADLY SINS

Peter Stanford
Introduction

It was in an effort to discover the contemporary relevance of the seven deadly sins for Christians and for a wider society that the *Catholic Herald* approached a group of distinguished novelists in the autumn of 1989 with the idea of a series of short stories on the seven themes to be published the following year.

It was not principally a theological exercise. None of the writers would, I feel, claim to be theologians, but the stories, published in Lent 1990 and now collected here, do owe a debt to the theology of the Christian churches, if only for defining the seven sins.

Sin itself is a distinctly Christian notion. Most fundamental of all is the original sin of Adam in the Garden of Eden when he took and ate the forbidden fruit. According to Christian teaching, the stain of sin, of Adam's betrayal of God's love, is with all human beings. 'We are all in this one man (Adam), since we all were that one man who fell into sin,' wrote St Augustine, one of the most often quoted of early Christian oracles, in the fifth century.

Drawing up a list of the seven deadly sins – or capital sins as they are sometimes known from the Latin *caput* or 'chief', was a logical stage in the

11

growing awareness of the early Christian church of sinfulness. First references to the seven – pride, envy, anger, sloth, avarice, gluttony and lust – come with the birth of the monastic movement around the fourth century and the seven deadly sins are sometimes spoken of as being 'first framed in the cloisters of the eastern church'.

Official codification of the seven sins was undertaken by Pope Gregory the Great (590–604), himself the founder of six monasteries in Sicily and one in Rome. He defined the seven so that they would be 'able to serve as a classification of the normal perils of the soul in the ordinary conditions of life', and not merely as a list of the temptations that those in abbeys must resist.

It was also Gregory who decided on limiting the list to seven. There is a suggestion that the ascetic, John Cassian of Marseilles, another of the early movers of the monastic movement, argued for eight sins. But the number seven has always had a special significance for Christian teaching – the seven last words of Christ on the cross and the seven sleepers of Ephesus, put to slumber by God in a cave to protect them from a vengeful emperor, being just two examples of this tradition.

The seven deadly sins became the staple fare of sermons in the Middle Ages. They achieved prominence, according to their expounders, not because they were the most heinous of sins, but because they could be used to define an individual's relationship both with society around him or her and with God.

At the end of the thirteenth century in England, Archbishop Peckham (1279–1294) ordered every priest to preach on the seven deadly sins four times a year 'in vulgar tongue without any fantastical imagination or any manner (of) subtlety or curiosity'. To the original list of seven were added 'branches' — also to be inveighed against from the pulpit.

The thinking behind these 'branches', also called 'daughter sins' (an example of Christianity's propensity to unite the negative and the female in one breath), was that the main seven had a special power to lead men and women to commit additional misdemeanours, like magnets drawing others towards their own ends. Hence, around pride were grouped presumption, ambition, vainglory, boasting, hypocrisy, strife and disobedience. With gluttony went mental dullness, excessive talking, buffoonery, uncleanness of any kind and 'immediate hilarity'.

The seven deadly sins were counterbalanced by seven virtues. In place of pride, the Christian should aim for humility, generosity rather than avarice, purity not lust, brotherly and sisterly love not envy, temperance not gluttony, meekness not anger, and diligence not sloth.

Those who went through a Catholic school at the time when the old penny catechism still formed the basis for religious education with its rigid question and answer formula for all the issues likely to confront the young believer (Q. Who made me? A. God made me) will be familiar with the order in which the seven deadly sins appear in this book. It is the formula laid down by Gregory the Great 1,400 years ago. Significantly, lust comes at the very end of the list. Both modern society and the modern church might reflect on Gregory's wisdom. Sexual morality has become both a topic of boundless fascination bordering on prurience for the public, and the touchstone of orthodoxy for believers.

The Gregorian plan has a certain coherence. All

seven sins concern love in some form or other. Pride, envy, and anger might be grouped as sins where love is misplaced. They all work on the basis that the sinner hopes to gain some advantage by causing harm to others. Sloth stands alone as love directed towards a deserving object, but not given its proper measure. And then avarice, gluttony and lust, loosely speaking, are sins of excess of love, where too much corrupts and destroys.

But that is to anticipate our authors and what is to come. This is not the first time the seven deadly sins have been addressed in a contemporary manner. But I hope that the short story form is an enlightening and entertaining way of approaching the issue of personal and social morality. When the authors of this collection first discussed the project, we spoke of the stories being potentially akin to parables. Christ used parables to put across his teachings. Christian writers in the late twentieth century are in this collection examining an ancient teaching formula of his church as seen in the life of ordinary people.

It would be easy, of course, to draw up our own list of seven contemporary deadly sins. One author suggested nostalgia, another marginalisation, a third sexism. The possibilities are endless. Yet what makes this particular list of seven vices especially intriguing is that all have their attractive and temptingly legitimate expressions. Take pride, for example. Generations of schoolchildren have been told to take pride in their work, their appearance, their homework. Is that a sin? Or anger. How many times do our courts decide that a defendant was right to lose his or her temper, to be angry? Or gluttony. On *Desert Island Discs* recently, cookery expert Prue

14

Leith revealed that she considers only gluttons make good chefs. Or sloth. In the film *Gone With the Wind*, Scarlett O'Hara may be judged to have got her rightful come-uppance when Rhett Butler utters the immortal and slothful last words 'Frankly, my dear, I don't give a damn'.

Debatable examples, perhaps, but illustrations that the seven deadly sins can still refer to much that is about us, and can offer a framework as comprehensive in its coverage as any scheme we may care to draw up ourselves.

A note of thanks should be added, lest I be judged avaricious or gluttonous in claiming the credit for myself, to those who have given of their time and energies to make this collection possible: Otto Herschan, Rocco Forte, Joanna Moorhead, and Juliet Newport of Spire. And of course to our seven contributors who rose to the challenge of illustrating the sins in prose, and to Clara Vulliamy whose drawings add to this collection as they did to the *Catholic Herald* when the stories were first published.

Peter Stanford
Herald House
London
May 1990

PRIDE

1

Andrew Greeley
Pride Before a Fall

onsignor Joseph Meany reached out from the tomb in the spring of 1945 to prevent Rosie from planting the May crown on the head of the Virgin Mary. The Monsignor's ghost encountered a grimly determined exorcist – my mother, April Cronin O'Malley.

April *Mae* Cronin O'Malley.

'Unlike the Mercy Sisters,' my father would say, looking up from a blueprint or a drawing, 'old Joe Meany was well named'.

'Vangie!' My mother would protest the irreverence and uncharitableness and then laugh, thus honouring with deft economy the obligations of respect for the pastor, love for her husband, and truth.

Joseph Peter Meany was a tiny man, a shrivelled gnome, not much over five feet three, thin, bald, and, like my mother, near-sighted and too vain to wear glasses. He compensated for his height, so my father said, by communicating with mere mortals in a deep bass bellow.

He firmly believed, Dad also said, that within the boundaries of St Ursula he was God.

At least.

'Everyone,' Mom would sometimes protest with little conviction, 'thinks he's done such a splendid job as pastor'.

That observation was also true. Meany Meany, as we kids called him, was of that generation of Irish pastors who could have counted on the complete loyalty of the majority of his parishioners even if he had been caught committing fornication with Mother

19

Superior on the high altar during the Solemn Mass of Easter Sunday.

Incest even.

'Sure,' Dad would snort, 'it was a brilliant financial decision not to build the new church in 1937 because he thought prices were going down even more. Now we won't have the church till after the war is over. If then.'

My father had some interest in the topic. He had designed the long-awaited new church. For free. In the middle of the Great Depression.

I hated Monsignor, mostly because he had, I thought, cheated my father out of payment for his work. I did not feel the smallest hint of grief when he went to meet his maker because of a heart attack. He expired consuming his third Scotch in celebration of the death of Franklin Roosevelt.

'God knows the old man died happy,' John Raven, the young priest, said to my mother, 'but if they assign Joe and the President to the same section of purgatory, he'll ask for a transfer to hell.'

'Where he belongs,' I added piously.

'Chucky!' my mother protested. And then laughed.

'Like father, like son,' Father Raven noted.

'Look at the way he treated gold star families,' I pressed the point. 'He won't even come down from his office to tell them that they can't have a priest from outside the parish say the funeral Mass. Instead he makes you do it. And he doesn't even show up for the wake or funeral unless it's a rich family!'

'Chucky!' This time my mother's tone said I'd better shut up. Even at seventeen I had sense enough not to argue with such a tone in the voice of an Irishwoman.

Rarely did any parishioner who was not wealthy

speak to the pastor. He immured himself in his suite after Mass each day (at the most a seventeen-minute exercise) and descended only for meals. He would talk to no one in the rectory offices. Rarely did he attend wakes or funerals or weddings and never did he make a hospital visit. His curates had to make an appointment to talk to him, and sometimes they waited weeks.

He kept, locked in a sacristy safe, a special bottle of wine to be used only at his Masses, a much more tasty and expensive vintage than the wine assigned to the other priests. I speak as one who has sampled both, with more restraint I hasten to add than certain other altar boys (who depended on me to open the Monsignor's safe).

Monsignor Meany was convinced that John Raven's name was James and called him that, as in 'James, that car door ought not to be open. Take it off!'

So great was the power of the pastor's command that John Raven, as he later admitted, without any hesitation or reflection, drove the Monsignor's sturdy old LaSalle straight into the offending door and continued serenely down Division Street as the door bounced a couple of times on the bricks before it halted at a stop light.

'Serves the damn fool right!' the pastor crowed.

No one ever complained about damage to the car.

The other priests called Father Raven 'Jim' at the meals which the Monsignor attended.

The pastor thought that William McKinley was the last American President not to be tainted with Communist sympathies, took the biased news stories in the *Tribune* as Gospel truth, insisted that FDR was a Jew, opposed aid to 'Bloody England', became a fan of Father Couglin when the 'radio priest' turned anti-Semitic (the same time that my father made me stop selling Couglin's paper *Social Justice* after Mass on Sundays), and firmly believed that Roosevelt had conspired with the Japanese to launch the Pearl Harbor attack. He never spoke against the war, exactly; but whenever someone from the parish was killed in action he would mutter audibly, 'Another young man murdered by that Jew Roosevelt'.

He would have easily won re-election as pastor if such had been required. His fans pointed to the Monsignor's extraordinary personal piety, as evidenced, for example, by his pilgrimage to Lourdes in the spring of 1939. They did not add that on the same boat which he favoured with his presence the Monsignor shipped to France both his LaSalle and his housekeeper (I forget her real name, but we kids called her 'Mrs Meany Meany').

My father lamented that he got out of Europe before the war started in September. 'Hitler probably would have given him an Iron Cross.'

'Vangie!'

'With Oak Leaf Cluster!'

'They don't give oak leaves . . .' I began.

'Enough from both of you.'

Wisely we both lapsed into devout silence.

In Joseph Meany's religion there was only one sin – 'impurity'. It was denounced with great vigour on every possible occasion – with, need I add, not the slightest indication of what it consisted.

Hence his stern injunction to Sister Mary Admirabilis ('Mary Admiral' to us kids and then 'Mary War Admiral', after the Kentucky Derby winner) that only 'a young woman who is a paragon of purity may crown the Blessed Mother. We must not permit Our

Lady to be profaned by the touch of an immoral young woman.'

'One with breasts,' my elder sister Jane snorted. 'If Rosie didn't have boobs . . .'

'That's enough, young lady.' Mom didn't laugh, but she kind of smiled, proud of Rosie's emerging figure, as though she were her own daughter.

It was the middle of May, a week after VE day and the end of the war in Europe, Monsignor Meany was in his grave – and whatever realm of the hereafter to which the Divine Mercy had assigned him – and Monsignor Martin Francis 'Mugsy' Branigan had replaced him. In his middle forties then, Mugsy was already a legend: shortstop for the White Sox in 1916, superintendent of Catholic schools, devastating golfer, ardent Notre Dame fan, genial, charming, witty.

The red-faced, silver-haired Mugsy had been assigned to St Ursula with indecent haste.

'Old Joe is hardly cold in the ground,' Dad commented as he toasted (in absentia) the new pastor. There was always something to toast when he came home after the long ride from Fort Sheridan. 'I guess the Cardinal knows that he has a problem out here.'

So Monsignor Mugsy was ensconced in the great two-storey room in the front of the second floor of the rectory, the part which was covered with white stone. But Mary War Admiral had not yet extended diplomatic recognition to him. In the school the word of the late pastor was still law.

Even though, as John Raven remarked, there is no one deader than a dead priest.

So Mary War Admiral voided Rosemarie Helen Clancy's nearly unanimous election as May Queen by the eighth grade, in solemn conclave assembled, because she was not the 'kind of young woman who ought to be crowning the Holy Mother of God'.

She then appointed my sister Peg as Rosie's replacement. Peg would have won on her own – she never lost an election that I can remember – but she had determined that her inseparable friend Rosie was going to crown Mary, and that, Peg being her mother's daughter, was that.

When informed by Sister Mary War Admiral that she was to replace Rosie, Peg replied with characteristic quiet modesty, 'I'd kill myself first!'

My mother's reaction was that (a) she would go over to the convent and 'settle this problem' with Sister Mary Admirabilis, and (b) that I would accompany her.

'I will not visit the parish,' she insisted, 'unless I am accompanied by a man from my family.'

'I'm a short, red-haired, high school junior,' I pleaded.

'Your father's in Washington this week at some meeting with the War Department, young man, and you *will* come with me.'

'You don't need a man to ride the Central bus with you up to the Douglas Plant,' I countered.

'That's different. Besides, you're as bad as your father. You're dying to get into a fight. Now go wash your face and comb your hair.'

'My hair doesn't comb. Wire brush. Good for scraping paint. Bad for combing.'

'TRY!'

'Yes MA'AM.'

I kept my opinions on the May crowning to myself. Sister Mary War Admiral, I thought, might have a point. The word from Lake Delevan (alias Sin Lake) the previous summer was that for someone just entering eighth grade, Rosie Clancy was terribly 'fast'. Admittedly, 'fast' in those days was pretty slow by contemporary standards. But that was those days, not now.

At that time she and Peg were slipping quickly and gracefully – and disturbingly as far as I was concerned – into womanhood.

'They had their first periods the same week,' I heard Mom whisper to Dad one night after the Bing Crosby 'Kraft Musical Hall' while I was supposed to be sleeping in the enclosed front porch I shared with my little brother.

I still didn't know exactly what a period was, but I suspected that it meant more trouble for me.

Standing together whispering plots, schemes, tricks and God knows what else, they seemed almost like twins – same height, same slim, fascinating shapes, same dancing eyes, same piquant, impish faces. Like Mom, Peg was brown-tinged, eyes, hair, skin, an elegant countess emerging from chrysalis. Rosie was more classically Irish, milky skin that coloured quickly, jet-black hair, scorching blue eyes.

Peg was the more consistent and careful of the two. She worked at her grades and her violin with sombre determination. Her grace was languid and sinuous, a cougar slipping through the trees. She rarely charged into a situation – a snowball attack on an isolated boy (like me) – without first checking for an escape hatch or an avenue of retreat. Rosie was more the rushing timber wolf, attacking with wild fury, mocking laughter shattering the air. If Peg was a countess in the making, Rosie was a bomb thrower or revolutionary or wild bar-room dancer.

She might also have been, to give her fair credit, a

musical comedy singer; she had a clear, appealing voice, which, I was told to my disgust when I was constrained to sing with her at family celebrations, blended 'beautifully with yours, Chucky Ducky'.

Yuck, as my grandchildren would say.

I must give her due credit. If she and Peg tormented me by, for example, putting lingerie ads from *Life* in my religion textbook and stealing my football uniform the morning of a game, they also came to my aid when I was, or was thought to be, in trouble.

Once when I was in eighth grade two of the more rowdy of my classmates made some comments which indicated that Dad was a 'slacker' because he was stationed at Fort Sheridan. In fact he was the oldest serviceman from the parish. Moreover neither of their fathers was in the service.

Instead of pointing out these two truths I made some more generalised comments on their ancestry and on their relationship with their mothers.

And thus found myself on my back in the schoolyard gravel being pounded, not skilfully, perhaps, but vigorously.

Even one of them would have out-numbered me.

Suddenly two tiny fifth-grade she-demons charged to my rescue, kicking, clawing, screaming. My two assailants were then outnumbered – not counting me.

'Where did you guys learn those words?' I demanded.

'From listening to boys,' answered Peg, breathless but triumphant.

'Boys like you, Chucky Ducky,' Rosie added, her face crimson with the light of battle.

They then, without my knowledge, went to the rectory and enlisted John Raven's support. The two rowdies were put to work sweeping the parish hall, as Father Raven put it, 'till the day before the Last Judgment'.

Rosie was, or at least claimed to be, broken-hearted at her demotion by the War Admiral, much to my surprise since I would scarcely have thought of her as devout.

'I feel so sorry for Peg,' she told me. 'It's not fair to her.'

'It's not fair to you,' Peg snapped, 'is it, Chucky?'

'My position on Sister Mary War Admiral,' I observed, 'is well known.'

'Stop talking to the girls,' Mom intervened. 'We must settle this silly business tonight.'

So we sallied forth into the gentle May night, an ill-matched pair of warriors if there ever were such.

'Now please don't try to be funny,' Mom tried to sound severe, always a difficult task with her husband or her firstborn son.

'I'll be just like Dad.'

'That's what I'm afraid of.'

The war in Europe was over. Churchill's 'long night of barbarism' in Europe had ended. Some men were being released from the service. Dad expected an early discharge. We were destroying Japanese cities with fire bomb raids. They were wreaking havoc on our ships with their Kamikaze attacks. We had lost thirteen thousand men in the battle for Okinawa Jima. Mom was worried that I would be drafted when I graduated next year and would have to fight in the invasion of Japan, despite my plans to be a jet pilot. (A legitimate worry, as it turned out. If it had not been for the atomic bomb I would surely have ended up in the infantry. They didn't need pilots.) The cruiser *Indianapolis* was about to sail for Tinian (and

27

its own eventual destruction) with the first atomic bomb. Bing Crosby was singing that he wanted to 'ride to the ridge where the West commences and gaze at the moon till I lose my senses', so long as we undertook not to attempt to fence him in. A battle over a May crowning surely did not compare to the major events which were about to shape the new, more affluent, and more dangerous world.

But it was our battle.

The O'Malleys were 'active' Catholics as naturally as they breathed the air or played their musical instruments. Mom had been president of the altar guild. Dad was an usher, even in uniform. Jane had been vice-president of the High Club. I was sometime photographer in residence, and the always available altar boy to 'take' sudden funerals, unexpected war-time weddings, periods of adoration during 'forty hours', and six o'clock Mass on Sundays. When our finances improved – Dad's military pay and Mom's wages from the factory – we discussed together increasing our Sunday contribution.

We voted, over my objections, to quadruple the amount we gave. Dad insisted that the Sunday gift be anonymous because he didn't believe in the envelope system or the published list of contributions.

'Why give if we don't get credit?' I demanded, at least partially serious.

'Chucky!' the other five responded in dismay.

Despite the anonymity of our gifts we were still prominent members of the parish. Even Monsignor Meany almost came to our house for supper one night. So Sister Mary War Admiral must have known she was in for a fight.

I whistled 'Praise the Lord and pass the ammunition' as we walked up the steps to the convent.

28

'Hush,' Mom whispered; and then joined in with 'All aboard, we're not a goin' fishin'.'

'Praise the Lord and pass the ammunition and we'll all stay free,' we sang in presentable harmony as the light turned on above the convent steps.

'You're worse than your father,' she informed me when she managed to stop laughing.

There was a long delay before the door opened – it is an unwritten rule of the Catholic Church (as yet unrepealed) that no convent or rectory door can be opened without a maddening wait being imposed on the one who has disturbed ecclesiastical peace by ringing the bell.

Sister Mary Admiral did not answer the door, of course. Mothers Superior did not do that sort of thing. The nun who did answer, new since my days in grammar school, kept her eyes averted as she showed us into the parlour, furnished in the heavy, green style of pre-World War I with three Popes, looking appallingly feminine, watching us with pious simpers.

The nameless nun scurried back with a platter on which she had arrayed butter cookies, fudge, two small tumblers and a pitcher of lemonade.

'Don't eat them all, Chucky,' Mom warned me as we waited for Mother Superior to descend upon us.

'I won't,' I lied.

The convent cookies and fudge – reserved for visitors of special importance – were beyond reproach. I will confess, however, that I was the one responsible for the story that, when the lemonade had been sent to a chemist for analysis, he had reported with great regret that our poor horse was dying of incurable kidney disease.

'April dear, how wonderful to see you!' the War

Admiral came in swinging. 'You look wonderful. Painting aeroplanes certainly agrees with you.' She hugged Mom. 'And Charles – my how you've grown!'

I hadn't. But I did not reply because the last bit of fudge had followed the final cookie into my digestive tract.

The War Admiral hated my guts. She resented my endless presence with camera and flash bulb. She suspected, quite correctly, that I had coined her nickname. She also suspected, again correctly, that I had been responsible for pouring the curate's wine into the Monsignor's wine bottle. Finally she suspected, with monumental unfairness (and inaccuracy) that I had consumed most of the Monsignor's wine and thus was responsible for the necessity of filling the bottle with lesser wine.

'You look wonderful too, Sister.' Although Mom had blushed at the compliment, she was too cagey to be taken in by it. 'My husband is at the War Department this week, so my son has come with me.'

Actually Sister Mary Admirabilis looked terrible, as she always did. Like the late pastor, she was tiny and seemed deceptively frail. Her eyes darted nervously and her fingers twisted back and forth, perhaps because she did not bring to the parlour the little hand bell which she always carried 'on duty' – the kind of bell you used to ring on the counter of a hotel reception desk.

Most of the other nuns also carried little hand bells, on which they pounded anxiously when the natives became restless.

War Admiral launched her campaign quickly, hook nose almost bouncing against jutting chin as she spat out her carefully prepared lines.

'I'm so sorry about this little misunderstanding. Your precious Margaret Mary should be the one to crown the Blessed Mother. She is such a darling, so good and virtuous and popular. I often worry about her friendship with the Clancy child. I'm afraid that she's a bad influence. I hope you don't regret their friendship some day.'

You praise the daughter, you hint at the danger of the friend, you stir up a little guilt – classical Mother Superior manoeuvres. And how did my mother, soft, gentle, kindly April Cronin O'Malley, react?

April *Mae* Cronin O'Malley.

'Oh, Sister, I would be so unhappy if Peg did not graduate from St Ursula's next month, just as Jane and Chuck – uh, Charles here did.'

Oh, boy.

'But there's no question of that . . .'

Mom ignored her. 'The sisters out at Trinity did tell me that they'll accept her as a freshman with a music scholarship even if she doesn't graduate.'

'But . . .'

'And, as sad as it would be to break my husband's heart,' Mom seemed close to tears, 'I'll have to withdraw Peg from St Ursula's if she is put in this impossible situation.'

'She wouldn't come back to school anyway,' I added helpfully, licking the last trace of fudge from my lips.

'Shush, darling,' Mom murmured.

'Please yourself,' the Admiral took off her velvet gloves. 'If Margaret does not choose to accept the honour to which she has been appointed, we simply won't have a May crowning.'

'Please yourself, Sister,' Mom smiled sadly. 'My family will have no part of this unjust humiliation of Rosemarie.'

31

I began to hum mentally 'Let's remember Pearl Harbor as we did the Alamo'. This was a preliminary scrimmage. Mom was touching base before cornering Monsignor Mugsy.

'My dear,' the Admiral's voice was sweet and oily, 'we really can't let the Clancy girl crown Our Blessed Lady. Her father is a criminal and her mother – well, as I'm sure you know,' her voice sunk to a whisper, 'she drinks!'

'All the more reason to be charitable to Rosemarie.'

'Like Jesus to Mary Magdalene,' I added helpfully.

'Shush, darling.'

'Monsignor Meany established very firm rules for this honour.'

'Monsignor Meany is dead. God be good to him.'

'Cold in his grave,' I observed.

'His rules will remain in force as long as I am Superior.'

'Time for a change, I guess,' I murmured.

'You give me no choice but to visit Monsignor Branigan.'

'Please yourself.'

The warm night had turned frigid.

'I shall.'

'Don't say anything, dear,' Mom said as we walked down Menard Avenue to the front door of the rectory. 'Not a word.'

'Who, me?'

After the routine wait for the bell to be answered, we were admitted to a tiny office littered with baptismal books. Monsignor Branigan appeared almost at once, in black clerical suit, medium height, thick glasses, red face and broad smile.

'April Cronin!' he exclaimed, embracing her – unheard of behaviour from a priest in those days. 'Greetings and salutations! You look more beautiful than ever!'

'April *Mae* Cronin,' I observed.

They knew each other, did they? Sure they did. All South Side Irish knew one another.

I considered my mother, whom I had always thought of as pretty – a tall, thin, near-sighted refugee countess. Monsignor Mugsy was right. Without my having noticed it, she had, as she passed her fortieth birthday, become beautiful. The worry and the poverty of the Depression were over. She no longer had to send me to Liska's meat market to purchase twenty-eight cents of beef stew mince from which to make supper for six of us. Her husband was safe at Fort Sheridan. The war would soon be over. Her children were growing up. She was earning more money than she would have ever dreamed possible. She had put on enough weight so that curves had appeared under her grey suit. A distinguished countess now.

I glance at pictures I took of her at that time. Yes indeed, Monsignor Mugsy was right.

'Is this galoot yours?' he nodded at me.

'Sometimes she's not sure,' I responded.

'Vangie, uh, John is in Washington,' Mom explained.

'What grade are you in, son?'

'I'm a junior at Fenwick.'

'Do you play football?'

'Quarterback.'

'What string?'

'Fourth.'

'I thought there were only three strings.'

Monsignor Mugsy and I were hitting it off just fine.

'For me they made an exception.' I was not about to tell him that I was more mascot than player.

'Where are you going to college?'

'I've seen Knute Rockne All-American. Win one for the Gipper!'

'Great,' the Monsignor exclaimed. 'Now, April, what's on your mind?'

Mom told him.

'Dear God,' he breathed, and reclined in his swivel chair, 'How can we do things like this to people? Some day we're going to have to pay a terrible price.'

'Mary Magdalene . . .' I began.

'Shush, darling.'

'I hear that Old Man Clancy is something of a crook.' The Monsignor drummed his stubby fingers on the desk.

'A big crook,' I said.

'You two are willing to vouch for the poor little tyke?'

'Certainly,' Mom nodded vigorously. 'She's a lovely child.'

'You bet,' I perjured myself because I thought my life might depend on it.

'Well, that settles that . . . ah, Jack . . . don't try to sneak by. I suppose you know the O'Malleys?'

'I think so,' John Raven, golf clubs on his shoulder, grinned. 'The kid has a reputation for switching wine bottles; watch him.'

'Calumny.'

'I hear,' the pastor said, peering shrewdly over his thick bifocals, 'we have some trouble with the May crowning. Why don't you talk to Sister, Jack, and . . .'

Father Raven leaned against the door jamb. 'The smallest first grader has more clout with the War

34

Admiral than a curate has.' He chuckled. 'It's your fight, Mugsy.'

'And your parish,' I said.

Everyone ignored me.

The Monsignor threw up his hands, 'See what's happening to the Church, April? Curates won't do the pastor's dirty work for him any more. Well, go home and tell Peggy – I know which one she is, she looks like you did when you crowned the Blessed Mother at St Gabe's – that her friend will do the honours next week.'

When we arrived back at our tiny apartment three blocks south of the rectory on Menard, Peg hugged me enthusiastically, 'Oh, Chucky Ducky, you're wonderful.'

Rosie, her face crimson, considered doing the same thing but wisely judged from the expression on my face not to try. Instead, tears in her vast eyes, she said, 'Thank you.'

'It was all the good April,' I replied modestly. 'I just carried her bowling shoes.'

Parish reaction to Monsignor Branigan's intervention was mostly positive. The Clancy kid was too pretty for her own good and a little fast besides. However it was time someone put Sister Mary Admirabilis in her place.

Was there any complaint that April O'Malley had gone to the new pastor to overrule Mother Superior?

Certainly not. If you are April O'Malley, by definition, you can do no wrong.

The Sunday afternoon of the May crowning, in the basement gym which had been Meany Meany's bequest to the parish, the blue and white plaster statue (pseudo-Italian-Renaissance ugly) of the Mother of

Jesus was surrounded by a circle of six early pubescent girls dressed as though they were a wedding party and one pint-sized, red-haired photographer clutching his Argus C-3 and flash attachment.

The ceremony had begun with a 'living rosary' in the gravel-coated schoolyard next to the church. The student body was arranged in the form of a rosary, six children in each bead. At the head of the cross stood the May crowning party, Rosie in a white bridal dress, her four attendants in baby blue, and two of the tiniest First Communion tots in their veils carrying Rosie's train.

The recitation of the rosary moved from bead to bead, the kids in the bead saying the first part of the Pater or the Ave and the rest of the school responding, accompanied, with not too much enthusiasm, by parents who had come to the ceremony with about as much cheerfulness as that which marked their attendance at school music recitals.

I lurked on the fringes of the 'living rosary', automatically reciting the prayers and capturing with my camera the most comic expressions I could find. It wasn't hard to discover funny faces, especially when a warning breeze stirred the humid air and the bright sky turned dull grey.

The voices of seventh and eighth grade hinted at the possibility of adolescent bass. The younger kids chanted in a sing-song which might have been just right in a Tibetan monastery. The little kids piped like tiny, squeaking birds.

The spectacle was silly, phoney, artificial and, oddly, at the same time devout, impressive and memorable.

As we moved from the 'fourth glorious mystery, the Assumption of Mary into heaven' to the verses of the Lourdes Hymn, which would introduce the 'Fifth glorious mystery, the crowning of Mary as Queen of Heaven', the first faint drops of rain fell on the crowded schoolyard. The voices of mothers gasped in protest.

It was decision time. John Raven drifted over to the War Admiral, nodded towards the sky, and then towards the church. Fingers caressing her hand bell, she shook her head firmly. We would finish the rosary. God would not permit it to rain.

Father Raven raised an eyebrow at Mugsy, resplendent in the full choir robes of a domestic prelate.

'Looks as pretty,' my father had remarked of the robes, 'as doctoral robes from Harvard.'

Mugsy peered at the sky through his thick glasses, as if he really couldn't see that far, and nodded.

John Raven shrugged: you're the pastor, pastor.

Mugsy stepped to the primitive public address microphone and said, 'I think God wants us to go inside.'

Obediently the altar boys in white cassocks and red capes – cross bearer and two acolytes with candles long since extinguished by the stiffening wind – began to process towards the church. The girls in the crowning party fell in behind.

The War Admiral's bell rang out in protest. Several other bells responded. A couple of nuns rushed forward and pushed the kids in the first decade of the rosary into line behind the altar boys: the rosary would unlink itself into a straight processional line, with the crowning party at the very end, like it was supposed to be, instead of at the beginning.

In which position it was most likely to be drenched, since the rain clouds were closing in on us.

37

I snapped a wonderful shot of the War Admiral twisting a little girl's shoulder back in line and another of her shoving Peg to a dead halt as my sister challenged the ringing of the bells and began to cut in front of the procession and dodge the raindrops which were even now falling rapidly.

Irresistible force met immovable object.

The conundrum was resolved by the push of parents. Not bound by the wishes of Mother Superior they rushed for the church door – despite the outraged cries of the hand bells.

Peg simply ducked around the War Admiral, snatched up into her arms one of the First Communion tots and, followed by Rosie, who had seized the other tot, raced for the church door in the midst of a crowd of parents.

I still have the prints on my desk as I write this story. Peg was not to be stopped.

God may not have been sufficiently afraid of the War Admiral to hold off the rain. But He (or She, if you wish) was enough enchanted by Peg to stay the shower until the crowning party had pushed its way into the shelter of the church.

Peg reassembled her crew in the vestibule at the foot of the steps leading to the basement church, waited till everyone was inside and then led the crowning party solemnly down the aisle towards the altar.

The nuns were too busy pushing and shoving kids and glaring at parents in a doomed effort to restore the 'ranks' to cope with a determined young woman who knew exactly what she intended to do.

Peg would have made a good Mother Superior in her own right.

Doubtless given a signal by John Raven, the organ

struck up a chintzy version of Elgar's 'Pomp and Circumstance', an exaggeration if there ever was one for this scene.

Only about half the school kids were soaking wet when they finally struggled into their pews. The War Admiral's determined efforts to restore order had deprived the kids of the 'sense to come in out of the rain'!

If Sister says you stay out in the rain, then you stay out in the rain.

All the nuns had miraculously produced umbrellas from the folds of their black robes and had stayed dry if not cool.

When the Admiral and her aides could turn their attention to the crowning party, Peg had herded them safely to the front of the church, where they waited patiently under the protection of Monsignor Branigan and Father Raven – and naturally in the presence of your, and my, favourite redhead photo journalist.

I still laugh at the pictures of the nuns turning misfortune into calamity.

Monsignor nodded to the younger priest, who strolled over to the lectern which served as a pulpit and began.

'To make up for the rain, we will have a very short sermon. My text seems appropriate for the circumstances, "Man proposes, God disposes" – I almost said "Sister proposes, God disposes!"'

Laughter broke the tension in the congregation and drowned the clanging hand bells. We were no longer wet and angry; we were wet and giddy.

I could imagine Mom and Dad arguing whether Father Raven had gone 'too far'. Mom would giggle and lose the argument.

The air was thick with spring humidity, girlish perfume, and the scent of mums, always favoured by the War Admiral because, as I had argued, they reminded her of funeral homes.

The crowning party fidgeted through the five minute and thirty second sermon. Eighth grade girls were too young for such finery, some of them not physically mature enough to wear it and all of them not emotionally mature enough.

Peg, however, looked like a youthful queen empress, albeit a self-satisfied one.

And Rosie?

She was shaking nervously and deadly pale.

And, yes, I'll have to admit it, gorgeous.

She kept glancing anxiously at me, as if I were supposed to provide reassurance.

I ignored her, naturally. Well, I did smile at her once. I might even have winked, because she grinned quickly and seemed to calm down.

The sanctuary of the 'basement church' was in fact a stage. The statue of Mary had been moved for the event to the front of the stage on the left (or 'epistle') side. A dubious step-ladder, draped in white, leaned against the pedestal. Of all those in church only the statue was not sweating.

After the sermon it was time for the congregation to belt out 'Bring flowers of the rarest' from 'garden and woodland and hillside and dale' as I remember the lyrics. Rosie bounded up the shaky white ladder, still the rushing timber wolf. The ladder, next to my shoulder, trembled.

Anyone who attended such spring rituals in those days will remember that the congregation was required to sing twice, 'Oh Mary, we crown thee with blossoms today, queen of the angels, queen of the

May!' During the second refrain, much louder than the first (which itself was pretty loud), the ring of flowers was placed on the head of the statue.

I had been charged to take 'a truly good picture, darling. For her parents, who won't be able to come'. Given the state of flash bulb technology in those days, that meant I had one chance and one only.

Just as Rosie raised the circle of blossoms I saw an absolutely perfect shot frozen in my viewfinder. I pushed the shutter button, the bulb exploded, the ladder swayed, and Rosemarie Helen Clancy fell off it.

On me.

I found myself, dazed and sore, on the sanctuary floor, buried in a swirl of bridal lace and disordered feminine limbs.

'Are you all right?' she demanded. 'Did I hurt you?'

'I'm dead, you clumsy goof.'

'It's all your fault,' Peg snarled pulling Rosie off me. 'You exploded that flash thing deliberately.'

I struggled to my feet to be greeted by an explosion of laughter.

What's so funny, I wondered as every hand bell in every nunnish hand in the church clanged in dismay.

Then I felt the flowers on my head. Rosie had crowned not the Blessed Mother, but me.

Even the frightened little train bearers were snickering.

I knew I had better rise to the occasion or I was dead in the neighbourhood and at Fenwick High School.

For ever and ever.

Amen.

So I bowed deeply to the giggling Rosie, and with a single motion swept the flowers off my wire-brush hair and into her hand. She bowed back.

She may have winked too, for which God forgive her.

These days Catholic congregations applaud in church on almost any occasion, even for that rare event, the good sermon. In those days applause in the sacred confines was unthinkable.

None the less, led by Monsignor Branigan and Father Raven, the whole church applauded.

Except for the nuns who were pounding frantically on their hand bells.

Rosie looped the somewhat battered crown around her fingers and joined the applause.

Then someone, my mother, I'm sure, began, 'Oh Mary, we crown thee with blossoms today . . .'

Rosie darted up the ladder just in time to put the crown where it belonged. As she turned to descend the ladder tottered again. I steadied it with my left hand and helped her down with my right.

She blushed and smiled at me.

And owned the whole world.

There was, God help me and the bell pounding nuns, more applause.

Rosie raised her right hand shyly, acknowledging the acclaim.

The Monsignor stepped to the lectern.

'I think we'd better quit when we're ahead.'

More laughter. Oh Lord, we were giddy.

'Father Raven, who has better eyes than I have,' he continued, 'tells me that the rain has stopped. So we'll skip Benediction of the Blessed Sacrament and end the service now, with special congratulations to the May crowner and her, uh, agile court. First we'll let you parents out of church, then our bright young altar boys will lead the schoolchildren out, then, Chucky, you can lead out the wedding, uh, crowning party. It won't be necessary for the children to go to their classrooms. We want to get everyone home before the rains start again.'

It was a total rout for the War Admiral. To dismiss the kids from church without requiring that they return to their classrooms was to undo the work of Creation and unleash the forces of Chaos and Disorder, indeed to invite the gates of hell to triumph against the Church.

The clanging hand bells displayed a remarkable lack of spirit.

Afterwards, back in our apartment, the sun shining brightly again, Mom insisted that I was hero of the day. Peg did a complete turn around, a tactic at which she excelled, and told everyone that 'Rosie would have been badly hurt if Chucky hadn't caught her', a generous description of my role.

Dad, returned from Washington in time for the show, affirmed that at last St Ursula's had a real pastor.

'Joe Meany is now in his grave permanently.'

'And War Admiral has been put out to stud.'

I was old enough to know vaguely what that meant.

My prediction was accurate. The following year, Sister Angela Marie, even older, it was said, than the War Admiral, appeared at our parish and governed with happy laughter instead of a hand bell.

In the midst of the festivities I wondered whether in my eagerness to freeze what I saw in my viewfinder I might have brushed against the ladder.

And what was the instant I captured on my plus-X film?

That night, when the apartment had settled down, I crept off to my makeshift darkroom in the basement of our building. After developing the film and exposing the paper, I watched the magic instant come up in the print solution.

What I saw scared me: two shrewd young women, one of them recognisable as a marble statue only if you looked closely, making a deal, like a buyer and seller at the Maxwell Street flea market. Rosie was about to offer the crown in return for . . .

Well, it wasn't clear what she expected from the deal. But she expected something. No, she was confident she would get it.

I hung the picture to dry, thought about claiming that the film had been ruined, and then reluctantly decided that I wouldn't get away with it.

'You could call the picture,' Mom would say, 'the way *Time* magazine does, Rosemarie and friend.'

None of them would see the deal being consummated in the photo. They would say that it was all in my imagination.

ENVY

2

H. R. F. Keating
Death Hath Also This

Death hath also this . . . that it extinguisheth envy.
(Francis Bacon)

 he Chief Minister had been done to death. There
could be no possible doubt about it. Done to death
in Raj Bhavan, high above Bombay, airy residence of
the State Governor himself.

For a long moment Inspector Ghote stood staring
down at her body, stunned by what he had just come
upon. It was plain what must have happened. The
Chief Minister would have been waiting in this
almost featureless Visitors' Room to see the Governor. Most likely to discuss his known wish for the
great bridge she planned across the huge width of the
harbour, to be named after his late wife, famous for
her charity work. Waiting, she must have whiled
away the time leaning from the wide open window,
looking out at the Arabian Sea far below, its surface,
sparklingly blue today, dotted with the white sails of
tiny yachts out racing. And then, from behind, the
murderer would have come quietly in. Seeing her
suddenly at his mercy he must have taken from its
place on the wall one of the pair of curved, silk-
slitting Moghul swords, the room's sole decorative
feature, and delivered the single, swishing, deadly
blow.

One fearful gout of bright, fresh blood was splashed
across the rich lemon-yellow of her gold-bordered
sari. But the weapon? Nowhere to be seen. It must
have been hurled at once into the restless sea below.

Coming to his senses, Ghote gave way to a brief flick of fury that he himself – here in these august surroundings merely to deal with the theft of a valuable bangle of the Governor's daughter's, 'It would be an easy matter for you, Ghote,' the Assistant Commissioner, Crime Branch, had said, 'start surmising on the servants' – should have been the one to discover this monstrous act. Then he ran from the room into the offices of the secretariat beyond, swiftly commandeered a telephone and insisted on speaking to the Commissioner of Police himself. No less a person for a case as reverberating with momentous consequences.

In an extraordinarily short time the Commissioner, with Ghote's immediate boss, the Assistant Commissioner, plus his top team from Crime Branch, were there. The Governor himself, Vice-Admiral Mehta, had come to greet them, drained suddenly of every spark of the dashing vigour Ghote had been struck by when – could it have been only half an hour ago? – he had spoken to him about the theft.

Before long the Commissioner turned to Ghote.

'Inspector,' he said with abrupt sharpness, 'how was it you came to be here, in this room, to discover this?'

It seemed to Ghote, who never before had as much as spoken directly to the mighty figure of the Commissioner, that he was not only being asked the question but was also being somehow held primarily responsible for allowing the Chief Minister to be killed at all.

Words momentarily deserted him.

'Speak up, man, speak up,' the Assistant Commissioner, alert at the Commissioner's elbow, snapped out.

'Yes, sir. Yes. Sir, I am here investigating the theft of one bangle, diamond, from Miss Urmila Mehta. Sir, the Governor's daughter.'

'Inspector, I know damn well Miss Mehta is the Governor's daughter. Come to the point. What brought you into this room at that time?'

'Sir, it is simple,' Ghote managed to bring out. 'My inquiries into the said theft had pointed to one Shantaram, a sweeper. He was having access to the bedroom of Miss Mehta from which jewellery in question was pilfered. I was informed also that the said fellow's duty this morning was the emptying of ashtrays, and I had seen one individual likely to be Shantaram just only going into this room itself.'

And at that the Assistant Commissioner pounced.

'The fellow was in here? Shortly before you were discovering the body only, Ghote? Did anyone else have access?'

'No, sir, no. I was myself in the corridor on the side of the private quarters. And on the other side, where the secretariat is, I have already found that no one had left the offices there.'

The Assistant Commissioner wheeled round to the Commissioner, face bright with triumph.

'Then, by God, sir,' he said, 'we have got our man.'

'Yes,' the Commissioner said. 'Yes, it looks as if you have, ACP. But wait a moment. Motive. What could be the fellow's motive?'

'Robbery, sir,' the ACP was quick to reply. 'Already Inspector Ghote from my team here had felt out and smelt out the fellow as a thief.'

But abruptly the Commissioner pursed his lips in doubt.

'No,' he said. 'No. Look at the body there. All that jewellery, and not a sign of any of it gone.'

49

It was true that the murdered Chief Minister still had decorating her person gold and diamonds in profusion, rings, hair ornaments, earrings, bangles, necklaces. Ghote recalled the name that was bandied around about her. Madam Claws. It had been bestowed not only because of her tenacious hold on power – she had been CM for an unprecedented five years, longer even than the Governor himself had been at Raj Bhavan – but also because, it was said, she was adept at 'reaping the loaves and fishes of high office'.

But the Assistant Commissioner was not to be deprived of his snap solution so easily.

'Well, sir,' he said, if with a deferential dip of his head, 'I am altogether appreciating your point. But look at it this way also. A fellow like this sweeper, Sundaram, Shantaram, whatever his name is, what feelings would he be having towards a lady such as the late lamented? Seeing the many signs of extreme wealth on her person itself? Why, sir, envy. Envy only. There is your motive. The fellow was altogether overwhelmed by envy.'

The ACP began darting glances here and there, already working out how the murderous sweeper might have made his escape. Waiting only for a nod of confirmation from the Commissioner to start the massive hunt.

But Ghote, standing attentively by, could not bring himself to agree with the ACP's theory, for all that it had his authority behind it. Would mere envy really have so inflamed Shantaram that he had committed murder? He felt unable to believe it, even though he had yet to come face to face with the fellow. He could believe that of nobody.

Should he voice his doubts? Dare he?

It seemed too that the Commissioner was more than half-convinced by the ACP's arguments. He was certainly putting forward no counter arguments. Yet surely there was something in the expression on his face that indicated he was not entirely won over. As, damn it, he should not be. To take the life of a fellow human being out of sheer envy of the possessions they had – it was non . . .

And then, suddenly flooding in, he knew that the idea was not nonsense after all. He himself had experienced, once, envy so inwardly devouring that he could have – yes, had he had the opportunity he might well have – killed because of it.

It had been in his first term at college. And the object that had out of sheer envy driven him, in thought, at least, to the point of murder had been a bicycle. Of course he had been young then. Young and apallingly unsure of himself. A raw papaya.

After weeks of footing it to lectures through the city streets day after day, bus fares being out of his reach, he had seen advertised on a college noticeboard a bicycle just within his means. When he came to inspect the machine he had realised why it was going so cheaply. It was as ancient almost as the venerable British-built college buildings themselves, and equally out of repair. But he found it would go, if not without sudden alarming internal slippages, and had stumped up for it, only at once to be confronted with the machine owned by Edul Pochkhanawala, the richest boy in his batch.

That machine had been everything a bicycle could be. Low-slung racing handlebars, three-speed gears – in those days the best there was – chromium glinting everywhere, little horn as well as the bell, leather saddlebag in gleaming black. And he had envied it.

51

He had envied Pochkhanawala, who besides being so well-off was a thorough duffer. Within days he had convinced himself that anyone who could never answer a question in class did not deserve to have such an easy, such a glorious, means of transport.

And his envy had grown, had grown and grown. Wherever he had gone in college he had seemed to see Pochkhanawala, sitting astride the narrow racing saddle of that shiny, well-oiled machine, twirling and whirling with insolent ease, catching the glances of the girls, however modest and covert, carelessly accepting the admiration of the boys.

Before very long – he remembered vividly, horribly vividly now – he had been unable to think of anything else but Pochkhanawala's bicycle. His work had suffered. He too had begun to be unable to answer questions in class. He had lain awake long into the night, night after night, tossing over elaborate plans somehow to possess that machine. He would steal it. He would steal it and paint it another colour and Pochkhanawala, the stupid fool, would never recognise it. He would wait for his moment – it would somehow come – and push Pochkhanawala under a lumbering bus while contriving to rescue the magic bicycle unscathed. Somehow, somehow, he would one day find himself astride that machine, cutting lazy arcs below the college steps while the girls in their array of multi-coloured saris looked on and nudged each other.

In the end he had rid himself of the obsession. Or, rather, he had been lucky enough to have had it knocked out of him. He had been summoned to the Principal's office and had been told his work had become so poor that he was to be superannuated. The shock had done it. He had seen in an instant all his hopes, all his parents' hopes, tumble in ruin. He had pleaded and pleaded then, and been given one more chance. And after that he had managed to fight the evil thing down, though for weeks afterwards he had lived in a state of dull emptiness. The memory of it came back echoingly to him now. The long, long weeks of utterly dull blankness. Of automaton life.

But, he had no doubt of this: envy for him then had been truly an evil thing.

Yes, it was after all possible that the sweeper, eaten by an equal obsession, could have seized that ready-to-hand, dazzlingly sharp sword and killed with it.

'Sir, sir,' he almost shouted, stepping eagerly forward. 'Sir, that is true and also no one except for Sweeper Shantaram was having access to this room while Chief Ministerji was waiting here.'

But the moment he had made the declaration, which as it had come into his head he had believed to be an absolute fact, he realised that it was not so. And, worse, far worse, the sole other person who had had access to the room had been someone of almost equal importance to the Chief Minister. None other than her party colleague, long kept out of office, her great rival, the immensely influential head of the sugar growers' lobby, B. G. Patil, known far and wide simply as BG.

And, yet worse, it was he himself who was the sole witness to the fact that these two, one so high, the other so low, were the only people who could have entered the Visitors' Room unseen and committed the crime.

He had in fact just glimpsed Shantaram, a figure in baggy khaki uniform, a chequered cloth across his shoulder and a bright red plastic pail in his other hand, as he had entered the room. But, busy at the other end of the long corridor leading past the Governor's office, making notes of what Miss Mehta had just told him in the private quarters about the number and disposition of diamonds in her stolen bangle, he had not at once followed the fellow. As much as seven or eight minutes had probably passed while, head buried in his notebook, he had made sure he had written down every particular of Miss Mehta's description. So he had not arrived at the murder scene until Shantaram had gone.

If, in fact, the murderer had been Shantaram. If, in fact, Shantaram had not already emptied the room's ashtrays and had gone out at the other side, an almost unnoticed presence, leaving the Chief Minister still staring out of the window at the little white-sailed yachts darting about far below. Because it was perfectly possible that after Shantaram had gone B. G. Patil had come in through the same door. Because no sooner had he himself recovered from his stunned reaction to finding the Chief Minister lying there dead, and hurried to telephone, than he had seen BG standing all alone in the small lobby directly outside. Had seen him and not seen him.

At that moment, able to think of nothing but getting to the telephone, he had scarcely taken in the sight, familiar from a thousand press photographs, of the waddlingly fat, white-clad, Gandhi-capped politician, huge jowly face ever dark with wrath, blubber lips constantly pushed forward in inflexible determination. He had even, in the rush and excitement of making his call to the Commissioner, of going back to the Governor's own office to inform him of what had happened, of hurrying once more to the murder scene to make sure no evidence was disturbed, totally forgotten that he had for that one short moment seen BG.

But now the sight of the man came fully, glaringly, back to him. Was it that he had actually set eyes on a murderer within moments of committing his crime?

But should he say what he had seen? After all, was it really likely that someone as much a public figure as BG, the man who had so often been within an ace of getting the Chief Minister's chair, would take recourse to crude violence? Then, too, BG was a person of influence. Within days now, with the death of the Chief Minister, he might well be filling that office. If he learnt then that a pipsqueak inspector from Crime Branch had accused him of murder, a posting to the most obscure and unpleasant police station in the country would be the least that awaited.

But BG had been outside the murder room only moments after the crime. He had.

He produced a tremendous ratcheting cough.

'Sir,' he hoarsely got out, putting himself directly nose-to-nose in front of the Commissioner. 'Sir, it – it is my bounden duty to report, sir, that – sir, I was forgetting that Mr B. G. Patil himself had access to this room at the time of the murder also. Sir, he also had opportunity.'

He did not know what he had expected. A blast of anger? A swift frown of cold ridicule? But what he saw on the Commissioner's face was a gradually dawning look of deep interest. It was followed by an expression, fleetingly there, that he could only liken to what he imagined might come on to the face of a shikari out after a man-eating tiger when the beast came at last within his sights.

The Commissioner turned at once to the ACP.

'Well,' he said, 'this puts a very different complexion on matters, eh?'

But the ACP was not going to see his pet theory go under so easily.

'Yes, sir, I am seeing that,' he said. 'But, all the same, there is still the question of motive. Such a person as BG himself . . .'

The Commissioner gave a grunt of a laugh.

'Envy, ACP, envy,' he said. 'You were saying it yourself. And who would envy the late CM more than our friend B. G. Patil?'

'Nevertheless,' the ACP answered, 'when the two of them are, it seems, having equal opportunity, then the one I would be betting on would be the man who was altogether lowest in the scale. And who no doubt is now half-way back to his native place.'

With that he gave Ghote a glance that boded him little good. He was, he saw with a sudden inward sinking, about to be labelled in his superior's eyes at least as the man who had let the murderer of the Chief Minister get clean away.

But the Commissioner had had another thought.

'You say you saw BG, Inspector, standing just outside here after you had seen the body? After the murder?'

'Yes, sir, yes.'

'Then, damn it, as likely as not, the man is still here. Come on, ACP, we are going to have a talk with Mr B. G. Patil.'

In a moment the two of them had left the room.

Ghote did not know whether to follow or to stay where he was. The team from Crime Branch had not completed their photographing and measuring, but it was not his duty to supervise them. Yet neither was it up to him to assist in the questioning of B. G. Patil. Thank goodness.

He hovered, glad only to note that the Governor too seemed as undecided. Eventually the pair of them stationed themselves near where the single remaining Moghul sword hung from the wall, alternately looking at the men working round the body and looking away.

But before the Commissioner and the Assistant Commissioner showed any sign of returning – was BG already under arrest; had he under that combined pressure instantly confessed? – the Crime Branch team completed their tasks. They looked at one another, looked round for the Commissioner, shrugged, and with muttered exchanges of comments lifted the body on to the stretcher they had brought and, without much ceremony, left.

Ghote hoped that, as they opened the door leading to the secretariat and the side entrance to the big house, he might get a glimpse of the Commissioner and BG in the lobby there and be able to form some opinion of how the interrogation was going. Would he see a chastened, disgraced figure ready to be led to a cell? Or would he see a look of fury on that round, fat, puffy-lipped face that would mean that a certain inspector who had dared to hint that a future Chief Minister had committed a foul crime was shortly to find his career over?

But, as far as he could make out as the stretcher with the body on it was manoeuvred through the door, there was nobody immediately outside. Probably the Commissioner had sought somewhere more private to ask BG the difficult questions he wanted answers to. The best place, no doubt, would have been the Governor's own office, just through the door into

57

the private quarter. But presumably the Commissioner had not wanted to give BG a chance, as they went back through the Visitors Room, of fixing on any details of the scene that might help him concoct some sort of alibi.

The door closed behind the departing team. Ghote looked at the Governor. He in his turn was staring almost sightlessly towards the open window at the other side of the room, though he could not have been seeing the blue sea beneath and the gay little yachts. What to do now? Should he, in his turn, quietly leave? Or should he say something to the Governor?

But what was there to say?

For a long minute, for two, he stood where he was, his mind made blank by the sheer awkwardness of his predicament.

Then at last he turned to leave, determined to scuttle away no matter what the great man beside him, alone in this room where such a terrible event had occurred, might think. And, at the very instant his eyes left the Governor's face, he realised that he had after all got something to say to this sea-hawk of old, who had for so many years watched over Bombay and all Maharashtra beyond from this high perch of his. It had come into his mind in a single rush of rapidly rearranged knowledge. Something more loomingly important than anything he had already had to bring himself to come out with during the whole last appalling hour.

Something he did not know how he was going to say, but something that had to be said. Had to be.

He turned back.

'Sir,' he said, his voice loud in the big, empty room. 'Sir, why was it that you were killing the Chief Minister?'

There. It was said.

He did not expect any indignant denial. He knew too surely the actual facts of it all. But he hurried on nevertheless, in a rush of jabbered words.

'Sir, was it, as I am thinking, because for years you had looked on at your victim with envy? With envy itself? Sir, were you seeing all that time a person who was able to wield the power that you yourself had once had, the power to order such things as the building of great bridges? A power such as you had when you were commanding ships but have had no more now for many years?'

The stiff-backed old sailor turned slowly towards him.

'How did you know, Inspector?' he asked. 'How did you know? Yes, I envied that woman. She was able to do things, to give orders and to see things happening because of them, and I was stuck up here. Powerless, feeble, washed-out. Why, even my wife, my late wife, was able to achieve more, in the way of her charities, than I was.'

'Yes, sir.'

'But how did you know that? How? Here was I standing wondering at what moment I should confess to it all, as I knew sooner or later that I must, before I . . . But I thought that without my confession none of you police wallas, high or low, would ever suspect what had happened in that one moment of madness that came over me. So how was it you guessed?'

'Well, sir,' Ghote said, painfully answering, as he thought of how the Governor would be arrested, be led away in ignominy to a cell, be tried for his life. 'It was Number One: you could most easily have come from your office in the corridor outside, perhaps with just only the intention to lead Chief Ministerji back with you. I was myself standing at that time beside the door from the private quarters, yes, but I was altogether concentrating on what I was writing in my notebook. You could have come in here unobserved by me, done the deed in ten to fifteen seconds only, and gone back into your office once more.'

'Was that all, Inspector? Only that?'

'No, sir. Knowing that was possible would not at all have been enough. Not to make me think the Governor of Maharashtra could be a murderer also.'

'So what else?'

'Sir, Number Two: there was the look you were having on your face, sir. It was a look of emptiness. I had seen it all the time there after I had told you that the CM had been killed. At first I was thinking it was shock only, and very much of contrast to the way you were looking when I was speaking with you earlier about your daughter's bangle. But then, just only now, I was realising it was something else.'

'Something else, Inspector?'

'Yes, sir. It was the look of a person who for a long, long while had been prey to the sin of envy and knew now that the subject of his envy was gone for ever. It was one hundred per cent emptiness, sir. Something that, in my own way as a young man, I was once knowing myself.'

The Governor gravely inclined his head.

'Yes, you saw it all right, Inspector,' he said. 'Emptiness. Utter emptiness. And that is all I have before me now. Emptiness.'

And then, with an access of rocket energy that took Ghote completely by surprise, the old sea-hawk whirled, seized from the wall behind him the pair to the sword with which he had killed the woman he had so obsessively envied and drew it searingly across his own throat.

The shrieking gasp Ghote was unable to restrain brought the Commissioner and the ACP rushing in once more, with fat, waddling, powerful B. G. Patil at their heels. They checked in the doorway.

'Sir,' Ghote said to the Commissioner, once he saw that he had fully taken in what lay in front of him. 'Sir, I regret to inform that Governorji himself confessed to me that it was he who had killed the Chief Minister. And thereupon he took his own life.'

'But – but – but why?' the Commissioner managed to bring out.

'Sir, envy. He was admitting he had always envied and envied a person with the power to be getting things done, as once he himself had had.'

'I suppose so. I suppose so, if that was what he said. But who would have believed it?'

'Well, sir,' Ghote said, 'envy, I am thinking, is not at all a good thing.'

But nobody seemed to have heard him.

ANGER

3

Kate Saunders
She Went of Her Own Accord

*E*verything had been fine, until Monica told Ida to sit down. Then Martin had shouted, 'Can't you ever stop being a doctor for one bloody minute?' and stomped off to the beach in one of his rages. The path was too steep and rocky for literal stomping, but despite his slithering feet and flailing arms, his whole demeanour had radiated giant sulks. Ida stood beside the heathery rocks which divided her mother-in-law's garden from the sheer drop down to the shore. She could see Martin parading across the sand below her, knowing he had an audience, and innocently convinced that he looked dignified.

'I'm sorry, Monica,' she said. 'I don't know what gets into him. He talks for days about coming here, and the minute he does, he gets angry with you.'

Monica was kneeling over one of her wind-blown herbaceous borders, neatly pulling weeds from the barren, sea-bleached soil. The late summer breeze lifted a loose hank of iron-grey hair across her cheek. She tucked it absently back into her bun with a hand encased in a huge gardening gauntlet.

'Goodness, don't worry about me. I'm used to it.'

Ida was getting dizzy. She did not mind heights, but her pregnancy made her less confident about her balance. She retreated a couple of steps.

'What was it all about? What did you say? I never understand what sets him off.'

'He's been angry with me ever since I stopped breast-feeding him,' Monica said. 'Don't you know that all men are angry with their mothers?'

'Why?'

'Dereliction of duty.'

'But you've been wonderful! He boasts about you at dinner parties.'

Monica's trowel paused in the act of levering out a rock. 'Does he?' She sounded amused.

'It impresses women no end. He tells them how you never gave up being a doctor when you got married, and how marvellously you ran the practice as a single parent, after Leonard left you. He's really terrifically proud of you,' Ida paused, feeling this needed a qualifier, 'in a way.'

'Oh.' Monica swung back to rest on her heels, and dug the rest of the rock out with her earthy-gloved fingers. 'How are you, anyway? I never have a chance to ask, when he's around.'

'I'm fine. It's – it's not that he doesn't care about me, you know.'

'I know,' Monica said mildly. 'I should have been concerned about his health first, even though there is nothing apparently wrong with him. But he's not the one carrying the baby. That makes them furious too.'

Ida felt she should be loyal at this point. 'He says – I mean, he has a cold.'

'Oh dear. Why didn't he mention it?'

Ida knew that Martin would wish her to look reproachful. She tried, feeling silly. I have to be on his side, she thought, but if only Monica had been less honest, less reasonable. A little more sentimentality would have made things so much easier. She was the sort of doctor who called haemorrhoids 'piles' and told patients to bend over, while they were still twittering prudishly about trouble 'down below'.

'He was waiting for me to notice,' said Monica, reading her mind. 'I was supposed to tell him he was looking peaky. Remind me to feel his forehead anxiously later.'

She spoke with indulgent affection, completely without rancour, and they both laughed. 'Now sit down on the bench, Ida, or you'll get varicose veins in the backs of your knees.'

The use of a person's name during a conversation was Monica's version of an endearment, like 'dear' or 'darling'. Ida sat down, touched. She had always liked this gaunt, soldierly woman, with her weather-beaten, gypsy's face and crisp, incisive manner.

'I hardly recognise him sometimes, when we're down here,' she said. 'He's never like this at home – he's so gentle and considerate –'

'Ida,' Monica interrupted firmly, 'you don't have to make excuses for him. Mothers bring out the worst in men. The mother is the mainspring. Good or bad – everything comes from her. And since life is usually more bad than good, she becomes a focus for a man's anger. They have to blame someone.'

Ida remembered Martin telling her that Monica had been the first doctor in the area to refer people to therapists instead of handing out tranquillisers.

'Who do women blame?' she asked.

Monica went on briskly flicking out weeds with the point of her trowel. 'When something goes wrong, who do you blame?'

'Myself.'

'There you are. That's the difference between men and women.' She smiled. 'That'll be eight-and-six.'

'Do you miss the practice? We often worry that you might be lonely, now you've retired.'

Martin speculated on his mother's loneliness all the time, as if saying it often enough might make it come true.

'Heavens, no. I do locum work. Have to keep my hand in. I was brought up to believe that it was important to be useful. My parents' idea of usefulness for a woman was embroidering tray-cloths, mine was being a doctor, but the principle is the same. Do tell Martin not to worry. But what about you? No problems, I hope?'

'None at all,' Ida assured her. 'Six and a half months of pregnancy, straight out of the textbooks.'

'Old Mrs Prewett next door is knitting it a matinee jacket – thought I ought to warn you. Blue, of course. Her generation thinks it's rude not to assume the first will be a boy.'

Martin's shadow fell between them. He had recovered his temper.

'Talking about the baby? I knew you would be. No –' he raised his hand importantly, as if in court. 'Before you say anything, don't apologise. It's all right.'

Whistling, he went into the cottage, shaking sand out of his plimsolls.

'It's all right, he forgives me,' Monica said. 'This time.'

Martin's fits of anger with his mother were constant, but brief. The afternoon's squall cleared into an evening of fair weather. Ida felt cosy and loved over supper, and fond of Martin. His mother complained she could not build a decent fire, and he built one for her; a beautiful wood fire which took the edge off the September chill.

He had hit the seam of bantering amusement which brought out Monica at her best. They were a pair of adults, instead of a mother and her perpetual little boy. Ida did not care about being excluded from their ancient jokes. It was comforting. They were a family.

Monica mentioned a friend of hers who had gone to the West Indies.

'Did she go of her own accord?' asked Martin.

Ida, who had been half-dozing, started as they both hooted with laughter, and blinked at them like a bewildered owl.

'Sorry, darling, sorry,' said Martin. 'It's a dreadful old riddle – "My wife's gone to the West Indies" – "Jamaica?" – "No, she went of her own accord". It isn't funny!' he added triumphantly, seeing her feeble smile. 'No, but the point is, it came out of a Christmas cracker, and it somehow got into Mum's prayer-book, and fell out during the sermon –'

'And we became quite hysterical,' recalled Monica. 'Oh Martin, do you remember the year when all the jokes in the crackers were in French?'

'*Garçon! Garçon!*' cried Martin, '*Il y a une mouche dans ma soupe –*' and they were off again.

His face striped with firelight, Martin was a living ghost of Monica. His complexion was fair, and his hair mouse-brown, but they were both sinewy and spare, with watchful hawk's eyes. Ida fell into a pleasant, pregnant trance, wondering if her child would have them too. When she was in bed Martin brought her some cocoa and drew the curtains across the rattling window panes. The rough winds receded far, far out to sea.

'Do you see anything of Leonard?' Monica asked.

Martin's shoulders tensed, and Ida's spirits sank. They were sitting at one of the warped trestle tables outside the Old Ship Inn, drinking beer and eating the landlady's doorstep cheese and pickle sandwiches. The season was over, and the breeze had fangs, but silver sunlight was dancing on the caps of the waves. And now Monica had to spoil it – it really was her fault this time. She must know, Ida thought, how cross it made Martin to talk about his father.

'Sometimes.'

'How's Bernice?'

'She's fine. They both are.'

'I'm glad.'

Monica was heroically good about the woman who had stolen her husband all those years ago, but she never could see that her being good was not enough. Martin wanted her to be grieved and sorry. She had managed far too well without him.

'Their youngest girl has just got a job in a building society,' Martin said.

'Has she?' Monica vaguely sipped beer and looked out at the horizon.

'Not that you'd consider that much of an achievement,' Martin said bitterly. 'But it's not bad, when you've only got a couple of CSEs. Dad's pleased.'

'Oh, I am glad,' Monica said again.

A large seagull was strolling about on the next table. Ida found herself addressing it earnestly, 'Sandra is a Very Nice Girl.'

'Dad doesn't measure success by qualifications,' Martin's voice was aggressive and challenging.

'No, he never did,' said Monica. 'I like that in a man.'

'Do you? You amaze me, mother. How can you like it? That was the reason he took up with Bernice in the first place. Because she wasn't always making him feel small, and leaping out of bed in the middle of the night to deliver other people's babies. But let me tell

70

you – there's nothing wrong with being a woman like Bernice.'

'I didn't say there was,' Monica said soothingly. 'She's very nice, and she's made your father very happy.'

'Oh for God's sake!' snapped Martin, 'Stop lying! You're only trying to convince yourself, and it makes me sick. You think she's common, because she worked in a cake shop.'

Unfortunately – very unfortunately – this made Monica laugh. Martin was touchy about his stepmother, and even touchier about his three half-sisters. Monica's cleverness and independence had driven his father into giving Martin embarrassing siblings with bad perms, nasty accents and crossed-over teeth. He never could forgive her for that.

'Laughing,' he said. 'That's your reaction to everything, isn't it? Because it means you won't have to deal with emotions – you can just feel superior. God, no wonder he left you.'

'Please,' whispered Ida.

Monica glanced at her sympathetically, but Martin ignored her.

'The fact was, you put yourself above him, and above me.'

Ida winced, but Monica only said: 'It isn't good for you, Martin, this anger. It doesn't change anything. It certainly doesn't explain what you want from me, and it makes Ida miserable.'

'I don't want anything from you,' said Martin. 'Good thing, isn't it, because I never did get anything. You were doctor first and mother second.'

'She had to support you!' Ida blurted out.

There was always a moment when she was goaded into taking Monica's side. It was the lowest point of

71

every visit. Martin became white with fury; almost stifled by indignation at the injustice of women.

'You stay out of it. She didn't bring you up.'

'Martin,' Monica said warningly.

Something like triumph glittered in his eyes. 'Here it comes. Mustn't upset little Ida, because she's pregnant. You don't care about me at all, do you? It's been Ida – Ida – Ida ever since we arrived. Sit down, Ida dear. Do you need a cushion, Ida dear?'

Ida had a moment of detachment in which she noticed the invented endearments. Monica never called anyone 'dear', but in his corrosive anger he believed that his mother gave to his wife the doting affection that was rightfully his. She would have been quite sorry for him, if she had not had the eerie feeling that he was somehow enjoying himself. It was another score for him in the imaginary battle.

'What do I have to do before you take any notice of me?' he demanded, 'roll around in agony? Die?'

'Is there anything the matter with you?' asked Monica.

Martin summoned his vestigial cold, in such a white heat of belief that his voice began to rasp. 'I think I might have the flu –'

'I'll give you something for it –'

'Oh, please don't bother. I'll make an appointment at the surgery.'

'What do you want from her?' Ida shouted suddenly. 'What the hell has she done wrong, except work to support you because your father buggered off with some tart in a cake shop?'

She smacked her hand down on the wooden slats of the table, and her husband and his mother stared at her like a pair of strangers. Martin was in a cul-de-sac of rage now, with no path but absolute fury in front of him. He leapt up, dropping the crust of his sandwich on his foot. There was a dangerous moment of comedy when the bold seagull instantly swooped on it and pecked Martin's laces undone. Ida was so terrified of laughing, her heart contracted. Half her mind followed his predictable tirade.

'You're just the bloody same, both of you . . . all right, I'll leave you here . . . you can have a good laugh at me . . . I'm always in the way . . . I've just been in the way all my life . . . in the way of her wonderful caring bloody career . . .'

He stormed away across the quay, vanishing in the masts of the fishing boats. Ida felt a tissue being pushed into her hand, and she lifted it to wipe her eyes.

'I'm so sorry –'

'This really isn't good for you,' Monica observed.

'But what's the matter with him?'

'I believe it's something to do with never coming home to the smell of baking,' said Monica. 'Except he's far too intelligent to put it like that. It's rather awfully funny, isn't it, when you think of the tart in the cake shop?'

Ida wanted to go and look for Martin. She could not control a sneaking feeling that they owed him an apology. But Monica insisted on finishing her sandwich, and having a long conversation about tumours with the landlord of the Ship. They were still at the table when Martin returned, coughing and holding his throat. He drove them back to the cottage, as Keats on his deathbed might have driven Fanny Brawne and her mother around Hampstead.

If they had been alone Ida would have made kiss-it-better noises, but her sympathy had no value now. This was all for Monica's benefit.

'Martin, there's some Paracetamol in the bathroom,' she said. 'Do take some for that throat.' She smiled at them both. 'I wonder if there's enough light left to make it worth lifting the geraniums?'

They departed the next morning. Martin's anger was burning steadily, like a pilot light. Ida knew there was enough fuel to last them all the way to London.

'She's so cold,' he complained, heaving the bags into the car. 'Everything has to be rational. And love isn't rational.'

'Oh darling, how can you say she doesn't love you? It's just not true – you're so unfair to her. She adores seeing you. She's thrilled about the baby. What more do you expect?'

He fixed her with a cold, stubborn eye. 'When our child has a cold, will you tell it where you keep the Paracetamol, and go off to lift the geraniums?'

'Not when it's little, no. But you're a big boy now.'

'She was always like that. No wonder Dad couldn't stand it.' He kissed her forehead. 'God, I'm glad you're so sweet.'

Monica came out to wave them off. Ida noticed that she looked rather old, wrapping her cardigan tightly round her thin shoulders. Martin noticed her calm smile.

'Glad to get rid of me,' he muttered, jamming his foot down and backing out of the gate.

'Look out!' shrieked Ida, and the second she did so, an elephantine tractor crashed into the boot, hurling them into the windscreen. The world danced and span. Ida's bones leapt fiercely inside her skin. Time became nonsense, and she saw, in snatches of primitive home-movie, divided by intervals of blackness, Martin climbing out of the car unscathed, scrambling over the bonnet to get at her door. Wetness snaking from her forehead and dripping off the end of her nose. Monica running towards them, Monica shouting her name. Some blackness. Waking with her chin resting on the open glove-compartment, raising her head to hear Martin screaming: 'You're unnatural! You're a freak! I'm your son and you should run to me first! Me first! How do you know I'm all right?' More blackness, followed by profound nothing. But in between, a snapshot of Martin hitting Monica so hard that she toppled to the gravel like a ninepin.

Lavishly supplied with grapes and Lucozade, Ida lay in hospital, wanting for nothing. She had concussion, a partly-shaved head and nine stitches, and was under observation in a pleasant private room, because of the baby.

'All's well that ends well,' the nurse said complacently, listening to the baby's healthy heartbeat through a stethoscope, 'You'll be out tomorrow. Won't your husband be thrilled?'

Ida said nothing. Monica had not been to see her, and she was thinking. On the opposite wall above the sink there was a reproduction of a medieval Virgin and Child. The Virgin in her jewelled head-dress knelt in a daze of adoration before the cradle, her hands meekly folded in prayer.

'That's what he wants,' she thought. 'That's what they all think they have a right to.'

And she imagined herself kneeling before the bunny-painted cot in the nursery at home. For the first time, she hoped it would be a girl – or she would be another heartless mother, bringing up an angry man all by herself, and laying up a store of black eyes for when he was old enough to hit her.

The West Indian nurse straightened the bedclothes and ate one of the grapes. Ida suddenly wondered if she came from Jamaica, and whether she had gone of her own accord. An unholy desire to laugh covered a vastness of fear she did not wish to examine.

SLOTH

4

William Douglas Home
Perchance to Dream

His wife brought in his coffee then leaned forward, kissed him on the forehead and went upstairs with her mother's breakfast. He re-read the letter from the editor and then re-read it again, several times more. Then he picked up his notebook and attempted the requested contribution.

Once or twice his head drooped forward as he tried to come up with an idea for the story but he fought against this bravely, trying to ward off the somnolence that threatened every time he thought about the theme the editor had chosen for him.

A while later he was standing by his desk holding the telephone. But soon he sat down as the editor seemed disinclined to close the conversation.

'Any progress?' the editor asked, pausing for a moment, possibly (the author thought) to take a sip of coffee.

He seized the opportunity and intervened.

'I'm sorry, Robert,' he said, 'it's just not up my street. Not in any way at all. I've always thought the seven deadly sins were phoney anyway. I mean how can anybody limit deadly sin to seven when there are a lot more?'

'Such as?' asked the editor.

'I couldn't tell you off the cuff,' the author said, 'I'd have to think about it. Look, can I go and get my coffee, Robert, and ring you back as it's half-past ten and that's the time I have it every morning, never mind what's going on in my mind or my notebook?'

79

Robert slammed the telephone down and the author, as he did the same with his, thought, 'Poor chap, stuck for a contributor I would imagine.'

As he stood listening to the sound of the kettle, he thought, 'Let's see then, what are the other deadly sins? Lust's one, I know. And jealousy, I think. And greed, I shouldn't wonder. That makes three. Now for the other four. Dishonesty? Or, if it's not, it ought to be. We're getting on. And cheating at cards, surely. Six. Now what's the seventh?'

As the kettle clicked his wife came in carrying a tray which bore the remains of her mother's breakfast.

'How is she this morning, darling?' he asked.

'Much, much better,' said his wife.

She started putting dirty dishes in the washing-up machine. When she had finished, he said, 'Darling, can you spare a moment?'

'Sorry,' she said, turning towards the door, 'I'm giving Mummy a bath.' Then she looked back. 'Well, then, quickly, if you must,' she said.

He jumped in at the deep end. 'What the devil are the seven deadly sins?'

'I really don't know. And I must run Mummy's bath,' she said, and went out of the kitchen.

Picking up his coffee, he went over to his desk and dialled Robert's number.

'Robert,' he said, 'Jim again. I've just been thinking. I'm not too strong on the seven deadly what-nots. Could you spare a second to run through them or are you too busy? Thank you so much, Robert. Yes, I have.'

He took his pen out of his pocket.

'All right. Fire away. Ah yes, of course. Of course. That was the one I couldn't think of. And who's going to do the others? Good God! Good God! Good God! Good God! Good God! Good God! Well, I never – what a posh lot! And I'm down for sloth? Is that right? But I've never written a short story. Don't be lazy? I like that. I've been on this the whole damned morning since I got your letter! Watch it. I'm not in the mood for jokes. It's far too early in the morning. Anyway, I've got my mother-in-law staying, and I'll be sent to get another bottle of her cough-mixture, so let's not waste time. Now, listen, Robert! You want me to write a story about sloth. That's your position. And mine is that I don't want to. I know you don't like me saying that. But it's the truth, old boy. I just can't feel the slightest urge to do it. Not the slightest. In fact the whole idea bores me rigid. Sorry, Robert. I may as well be frank about it. I'm afraid the answer's No. I'm – hold on a second, Mary's saying something.'

Jim covered the mouthpiece. 'Yes, what is it darling?'

'Mummy's cough-mixture's run out,' she told him. 'Could you go and get another bottle?'

'When I've finished talking,' he replied.

'Who is it?' she asked.

'Robert,' he said.

'Robert?' she asked. 'What does he want?'

'A short story from me. Hold on just a minute, Robert. Mary's asking after you. Hold on. He'd like to say good morning to you, darling.'

Mary turned back from the door and took the telephone.

'Good morning, Robert,' she said. 'What are you up to with Jim? Oh, how exciting! Oh, dear, why not? But why? It sounds lovely. What? All right, I'll try to. But you know what he's like. Do you want to speak to him again? OK then, Robert. Yes. I'll tell him.'

Turning to Jim, as she rang off, she said, 'He wants you to ring him back if I make any progress.'

As he watched her putting back the telephone, Jim told her not to be so bossy.

'I'm not being bossy,' Mary replied. 'I'm just thinking it's extremely wet of you to say that you can't do it, when you haven't even tried.'

'I know I can't,' said Jim. 'And of course you know I can,' he added, with sarcasm in his voice.

'I know you ought at least to try,' said Mary, moving to the door. 'And so do you. And don't forget the cough-mixture.'

She went out. He looked after her and picked the telephone up.

'Could I speak to Robert Lightbody? Robert? It's Jim again. Look, I'll have a try, but don't blame me if it's a wash-out.'

He hung up and left the room to do his good deed for his mother-in-law.

Forty minutes later he was sitting in his armchair writing intermittently, then looking up and frowning and then writing intermittently again. He looked up once again, frowned deeply, tore the pages from the notebook that he had been writing on, went over to the desk and dropped them into the wastepaper basket.

Mary came in. 'Sorry, darling, where's the cough-mixture?'

'It's in the kitchen,' he said, shortly.

'What is the matter? Have you got stuck?' she asked.

'It's no damned good,' he said. 'And I'm ringing Robert up to tell him so.'

'Hold on a second,' she said, as she turned to leave the room, 'I'll give Mummy her cough-mixture, then I'll be back.'

He picked the telephone up and then put it back, picked up the basket and retrieved the pages from his notebook and then started to re-read them.

After a short while, he tore them into shreds and threw them back into the basket. Mary came in with a dictionary and sat down on the sofa.

'Now then let's just look up sloth and see if it'll help us,' she said with an air of finality. 'Sloth,' she read out. 'Laziness, sluggishness. A sluggish arboreal tropical American edentate. Spend time in sloth. Given to sloth, inactive, lazy. No teeth.'

'Stop it, darling,' he said, 'for God's sake. There's no point going on like that.'

'Listen to this: Sloth bear, a black Indian bear with prolonged snout and lips.'

Then she looked up. 'You never knew that, did you?'

'I don't think I've missed much,' he replied.

'But it's quite fascinating, darling,' she said. 'Specially that bit about them having no teeth.'

'What's so wonderful about that?' he asked.

'Well, just think how lovely that'd be to write about,' she said.

'What? Sloths having no teeth? Fascinating,' he said.

'Darling,' she said with excitement, 'think what a lovely story you could write about that,' warming to her theme. 'Say a baby sloth fell out of a tree – well, it says they are arboreal – and a small boy found it and took it home with him, and showed it to his father who's a dentist. Can't you see it, darling?'

'No, I can't,' he said. 'Even if I could, I'd rather not.'

83

'But it's a wonderful idea,' she said excitedly. 'And I'll tell you why. Because the little boy finds that he has to feed it on the softest things because it's got no teeth so he asks his father if he couldn't make Jim a plate? – he's called the baby sloth Jim, you see – and his father, who's the sweetest man and always has been, says, "Why not?" And so he makes Jim one – or rather two plates – one for his top jaw, the other for the bottom and they both fit perfectly. And then the little boy starts feeding him on harder things like boiled eggs and then fish and meat and cheese and everything.

'And then the baby sloth gets ill and would have died if the boy's mother hadn't thrown its plates away and put it back on to its normal diet just in time. And father didn't mind a bit because he loved the baby sloth as much as mother and the little boy did.

'And one day they took it out to see its parents and came back with them and all the other baby sloths and they all lived there ever after.

'And the father's practice grew and grew because his patients loved to sit and watch them through the window in the orchard all the time that he was working on their teeth.'

She looked up at Jim. 'Darling, isn't it exciting?' she asked.

'I think it's high time you went and gave your mother some more cough-mixture,' he said.

With that she closed the dictionary and left the study.

Jim sat thinking. After a few minutes, he picked up the telephone and dialled.

'Could I speak to Mr Robert Lightbody?' he asked. 'Robert, it's Jim again. Mary's just had an idea. About sloth. Yes. She says that I ought to write a story about sloths. What sort of story? I'll tell you.'

'Well, a baby sloth falls out of a tree and a small boy picks it up and takes it home. I'm cutting it down to the bare bones, Robert, OK? Right.

'He takes it back home. His father's a dentist. The boy feeds it on soft food. Then he suggests to father that he ought to make a plate for it – two rather – so that it can spread its diet wider, which he does. They fit, and so the little boy starts feeding it on every kind of thing – you name it and he gives it to it. Then it gets ill and it nearly dies.

'And so his mother – not the sloth's, the little boy's – decides to throw the plates away, which she does. So the little boy starts feeding it again on all the things that it eats normally like grass and leaves and all that sort of thing. And it recovers.

'Then they take it back to see its parents, and the parents and the other little sloths come home with them for good. And all his father's patients love them and they tell their friends and they all flock to him and he becomes a very rich man.

'Well, what do you think of that? You still there, Robert?'

Jim sat holding the receiver in his hand for a long time. Then Robert started to speak.

Jim listened for a time, then he said, 'Yes, I see. Not quite what you're looking for. I thought you'd say that. Don't I think what? The same as you do. Well, I did. But I'm not sure I do now. In fact I find it quite fascinating. Just as Mary – bless her – said I would. Still, if you think it's no good, let's forget it, shall we? So long Robert.'

He was about to replace the receiver when the editor spoke again.

'What's that, Robert? I see. All right then, I'll have a go at it. When do you want it by? The middle of next week. What day is it now? Tuesday. Good God! All right, Robert, I'll do my best. What's that? Good Lord, of course I won't be – no. It's up to you to print it or not. If you don't though, I'd like to think I'd get a little recognition for the work I've done.

'What? Yes of course I'll let you know if I don't do it. If I've not got into it by Saturday I'll ring you at home. And if you do print it, could I be anonymous? Why not? Well, they won't want to be. But I do. I see. Well, I'll ring you Saturday.'

He hung up, went back to his chair and started writing.

At precisely half-past ten on Saturday he put his pen back in its sheath, picked up his notebook and went over to his desk, picked up the telephone and dialled.

'Robert,' he said. 'Jim here. Just to say I've finished it and I'll post it Monday morning. OK? That is not for me to say. Well, good luck, Robert, and I hope you make the right decision. What's that? No, she hasn't. Am I going to let her? If it comes out, yes, of course. But, if it doesn't, no. Bye, Robert, have a nice weekend.'

He hung up, picked up a big envelope and started to fit in his contribution. Mary came in.

'Finished, darling?' she asked.

'Finished darling,' he replied.

'But you've not drunk it, darling,' Mary said as she went over to pick up the cup. 'And it's stone cold.'

He woke up with a start and looked down at the empty notebook on his knee.

'I'm sorry, darling,' he said, as she went out with the cup. Then he picked up the telephone and dialled.

'Could I speak to Robert Lightbody?' he said. There was a pause. 'Is that you, Robert? Jim here. Just to tell you I can't write that story for you. I really have thought about it. In fact I've just dreamed about it. Write what? My dream? But whatever for? Good God! Will you pay me for it even if you don't? I see. Right. I'll settle for that, Robert, just as long as it's incognito, if you decide to use it.'

He put down the telephone and went to boil the kettle for his coffee.

COVETOUSNESS

5

Morris West
Take Heed!

And Jesus said to them, 'Take heed, and beware of all covetousness . . .' And he told them a parable. (Luke 12:15–16 RSV)

I've given up asking people 'Do you remember?' I've had too many shocks recently, as fellows with grey hair and pot bellies, or matrons with marriageable daughters, remind me, 'For God's sake! I wasn't even born then!' So I won't ask whether you remember 1934.

I remember it, because I was then eighteen years old. I was on my first mission as a professed religious in the Congregation of the Brothers of the Christian Schools of Ireland, in one of the inner suburbs of Sydney. I was full of zeal and innocence, woefully ignorant of what was going on in the world – which, one way and another, was quite a lot.

The Japanese-installed Pu Yi puppet Emperor of Manchu Kuo, Russia and Finland signed a ten-year non-aggression pact. Hitler and Mussolini met in Venice. Chancellor Dollfuss was murdered in Austria. King Alexander of Yugoslavia was assassinated in Marseilles and Hitler was confirmed by plebiscite Führer of Germany. Marie Curie died, and, unbeknown to any of us, Sophia Loren was born.

I was teaching basic skills in reading, writing, mathematics, geography, social deportment and the rudiments of Christian belief to forty-odd third-graders, most of them from urban industrial areas, with a mixed population of Irish, Greek and Italian migrant stock. Our Community served three schools, and numbered, if my memory serves me right, some twenty-odd brothers, among them the subject of this cautionary tale, Brother Avellino.

He was a tubby fellow, with a bald pate and black eyes and an ever-ready smile. I still had the bloom of the novitiate on me and the veil of innocence draped over my head, so I missed the shrewdness in the eyes and the facile shift of the smile and the extraordinary mobility of his opinions – yea one moment, nay the next, a saving 'maybe' if the mood of the audience seemed uncertain. I also missed the cautionary comment of the Senior Member: 'Avellino? I've served three terms with him now, in three different Communities. Never tell him a secret that you don't want told all over town. He's everyone's man but always his own – and he's as shrewd as a Kerry horse-coper.'

Avellino taught the form above mine, so we worked in adjoining classrooms. Each of us had a choir in training for the City of Sydney Eisteddfod in which choirs and soloists from all over the state competed every year. We were considerate of each other. Each kept his classroom very quiet while the other was rehearsing his singers. We were also discreetly critical, noting examples of ragged phrasing, poor attack, bad intonation. I was too much the junior, too recently trained in monastic manners to announce my opinions; but, as the weeks passed, I began to nurture a fair hope that I might not only beat Avellino at choir work, but even have a chance of winning our section of the Eisteddfod.

There were no tape recorders in those days. We didn't even have a piano in the classroom. For four days a week we sang unaccompanied, using a pitch pipe and a tuning fork to set the key. On the fifth day we had an hour in the music room, with an accompanist. In between, I would run the pieces over and over in my head – an obsessional exercise in musical memory.

The obsession, however, ran more deeply and darkly than I dreamed. The Eisteddfod was a public competition, an open test of my untested abilities. I wanted desperately to qualify for the finals. Even if I didn't win, I wanted to be there, to step for a brief moment out of the anonymity of conventual life and have other people confirm to me who I was, or who I dreamed I might be.

Under the system then prevailing, I had been recruited as a postulant at the age of fourteen and had spent four years in tutelage before taking my first annual vows. Such identity as I had was uncertain and fragile. All my social reflexes were as conditioned as those of Pavlov's dogs. My convictions had been handed to me ready-made by a novice-master who, even in my most charitable recollection, remains a tyrant figure.

Came the day when I was absolutely convinced that I had a real chance at the prize. The Headmaster, who was also the Brother Superior of the Community, paid me one of his rare compliments. With an unexpected grace, Brother Avellino conceded defeat. His own group was no match for mine. He was withdrawing it from the competition.

From that moment I coveted the prize, with an urgency I would not have believed possible. My passion infected the choir itself and the whole class. We were an élite of the élite – almost as important as the school football team. We invented games for ourselves – a burst of four-part harmony in the middle of an arithmetic lesson, a round to finish an afternoon English period. It was all good clean fun and we knew, with the serenity of total faith, that the prize was just at our fingertips.

Then I fell sick, very sick. The doctor was called. He diagnosed double pneumonia. My monastic cell was at that time a glassed-in verandah, cold and draughty. Hurriedly, one of the other juniors was moved into it and I was lodged inside, to be cared for by the housekeeper who, whatever her nursing abilities, was certainly a cure for concupiscence! Those were the days before antibiotics – you see, the dates are significant! – so my recovery was slow. Brother Avellino took over my classes, managing some eighty boys like a roly-poly sentinel at the communicating door.

He took over my choir too, and in the evening bouts of fever I remember his voice, soothing as a sea breeze, delivering his reports: 'There's nothing to worry about. They're in splendid voice, singing like angels. All you have to do is get better and we'll walk away with the prize!'

I was sick. I was young and stupid. I was innocent still. I missed the plural pronoun 'we'. On the other hand, why should I have adverted to it anyway? A choir was a collective. A religious Community was a collective. 'I', so my masters had taught me, was a dangerous literal; all their training was designed to suppress it, debase it to petty currency.

So, full of faith and confidence, I moved from illness to convalescence. I saw no sinister possibilities in the fact that I was forbidden to return to the classroom for at least two weeks after my release from confinement. I knew I was weak and unsteady. I was happy in the fraternal support of the Community and the friendship of Brother Avellino in particular.

On the other hand, I wasn't too happy with the sounds I heard during choir practice. I knew Brother Avellino had a tin ear, but I was confident that with the Eisteddfod still a month away I could whip the group back into shape in a week. They had to present only two pieces. We had ample time to repolish the performance.

So I caught up on my reading, strolled in the garden, rested in the afternoons and joined the brothers for evening chapel. When the two weeks were up the doctor pronounced me fit for duty. I moved back to my old draughty verandah. The Brother Superior handed me a new teaching roster. It showed that I would take Brother Avellino's class for one period a day, while he took mine for choir practice. He had, it seemed, taken over the choir and would present it at the Eisteddfod.

I was devastated. I demanded to know why. The Brother Superior reminded me coldly that I was a man under obedience and he was not obliged to offer me any explanation for his actions. I protested that he owed me both courtesy and charity. His answer was curt. I was still a junior in religious life. I should remember the lessons of my novice-master and bow my neck under the yoke of discipline. I should never, never cling to anything so tightly that I would be unhappy to let it go. I should never covet anything so much that I would commit sin to get it. And I was in sin, was I not, however venially, for questioning the judgment of my lawful superior, for wanting the worldly satisfaction of a stage appearance, for lack of charity to Brother Avellino, who had shouldered the burden of my classes for nearly six weeks and had earned the right to this small concession on my part. I should go to the chapel, beg forgiveness for my faults and pray for light to understand the wisdom of what had been done.

My visit to the chapel produced a small light: a boyhood memory of my favourite aunt, who had kept house for her widowed father, an Irish police sergeant, and brought up my mother, two other sisters and a brother. To me she was and is a second mother – and if she's not in heaven I don't want to go there! Whatever small wisdom I have came from her.

'Morris, darlin',' she told me one day, 'never argue with the Irish! They're slippery as eels in a bucket and they've always got God on their side! So don't buy into their squabbles. Button your lip and walk away. You'll keep your dignity and save yourself a lot of heartache.'

That took care of the Brother Superior, with whom I knew I couldn't win anyway. It didn't answer the larger question about Brother Avellino. He and I were supposed to be brothers in a community; we were supposed to be living under a common rule; but clearly a different set of rules was being applied to him. In my folly, I decided to confront him. I wasn't about to demand the return of my choirmaster's baton, only to seek his personal explanation for what had happened.

Well, now! Eels in a bucket, was it? Kerry horse-coper, was it? This was the great Daniel O'Connell himself, back from the dead, eloquent with righteous amazement. Had he not tended me and done my work every long day of my illness? Had he not held my hand and mopped my brow while I babbled in the fever? Had I not pleaded with him to take over the baton and conduct the choir in a triumphal marching chorus to victory? He smote me hip and thigh with singulars and plurals. 'I said, you said, we agreed, and was it not so now? And for the sake of the boys that have put so much into this, should we not put an end to rivalry and confusion? Besides, I'm the senior and the more experienced and the better able to handle a public occasion. The Brother Superior himself recognised that.'

My sainted aunt was right. There was nothing for it but to button my lip and walk away, wrapping the last rags of my dignity around me. Still, my trials weren't over. Every day Brother Avellino walked into my classroom for choir practice, while I was shunted into his domain, out of sight but not out of earshot of my singers. Every day he offered his brightest smile and a variation on the same bit of blarney.

'You'll be keeping an ear cocked now, won't you? And if you hear anything that fails to please you, you'll let me know, won't you? They're still your boys. I try to make them feel that, and they do . . .'

After a week of it, I gave up listening. After two, I was past caring. When the choir was eliminated in the first audition, I managed to find enough grace to tell the boys it was a good try and enough irony to offer tea and aspirin to Avellino, who was taking to his bed with a migraine.

The Brother Superior, however, went public with lavish praises of what he called Avellino's splendid effort under difficult circumstances. He pointed out that my compliance had saved me from the great disappointment which Avellino was bearing valiantly in my place. I felt like throwing up. Instead, I poured out my anger to the Senior Member.

'Why is he acting like this? The competition's over. We lost. Why does he have to keep on justifying Avellino?'

The Senior Member studied me over the steel rims of his spectacles. He keened over me like a mourning dove. He quoted the Apocrypha at me.

'"Weep for the dead one because he has been taken from the light. Weep for the fool because he has no understanding." Where do you think you're living, boy? In Thomas More's Utopia? This is real life, the purgative way; and the sooner you wake up to it the better. But as to your question, don't you know there's an election coming up?'

'What election? I haven't heard of one.'

'Because you don't listen. You're so busy contemplating your own navel, you don't watch what's going on around you. These are elections to the Provincial Council, the governing body under which, believe it or not, you live!'

'I haven't seen a ballot paper.'

'But you wouldn't, would you, because you're a junior under temporary vows and you don't have voting rights. That's the constitution you chose to live under, but obviously nobody's directed your attention to its meanings!'

'But what's this got to do with Avellino and the Brother Superior?'

'Give me strength! The Brother Superior's a candidate for election. His nomination is in, signed by Brother Avellino and some others. Now does it make sense?'

'Not quite. What does Avellino get out of it – and don't tell me it's a choirmaster's baton!'

'Not at all. He fancies himself as a musician but he's got no talent for it. What he really wants is to be appointed a Superior and run his own Community. What quicker way to arrange it than to have a friend on the council?'

98

'That's despicable!' Even now I can hear the out-raged innocence in my voice. 'Canvassing for oneself or another is forbidden by the rules!'

'Is it now? So you're beginning to remember a few things! Sure it's forbidden, but that doesn't mean to say it's not practised – under another name. The idea disgusts you?' The Senior Member nodded placidly. 'But that's what happens when you want anything too much. You end up licking boots and backsides to get it. It's the way of the world, boy and if you think the world isn't here inside our own walls, you're too damned innocent for your own good!'

And there it was, plain as the nose on my face – and I'd have seen it if I'd looked in a mirror. I was just as guilty as they were, just as ridiculous in my search for a juvenile satisfaction, redress for petty wrong.

In one particular, however, I was different – not better, just different: I had not attempted to use the mechanisms of power to procure my own satisfaction or subdue an adversary who threatened me. I had not used them because I did not control them, as the Brother Superior did or, in his own degree, Brother Avellino. But the mechanisms existed. They could be used. They would be used. They had been used in my case.

As I look back now over a gap of fifty-six years, I see that moment as the beginning of the slow erosion of my convictions about the authenticity of my own vocation to religious life. For one thing, the life wasn't religious of itself, only in so far as its prac-titioners made it so. In another, my own innocence was spurious because it was untested. I was not a pilgrim in progress. I was a raw youth in flight from certain unpleasant realities in his life. I would not solve my problem by making other illusions out of other and harsher realities. It would take me a long and painful time to face the truth. At the end of that year I applied for a transfer to a different Community. The pilgrimage had just begun.

For a long time I could not rid myself of the presence of Brother Avellino. I knew him, or thought I knew him, for a trivial man who could neither harm me nor help me; but, every now and then, on the faces of total strangers, I would see his dark gypsy eyes studying me, his easy horse-coper's smile flashing at me. Inside the monastic walls and long afterwards outside them, his phantom presence was always associated with the same kind of experience. I would want something very badly – an assignment, a contract, an introduction. There would always be a horse-trader with Avellino's eyes and Avellino's smile, waiting to procure it for me – for minimal consideration, out of pure friendship or professional respect. Always my hackles would rise and I would become guarded and brusque. I wanted no bargains, just a fair deal at a fair market price, with no favours given and none owed. That was Avellino's first and worst legacy to me, a Homeric distrust of go-betweens and matchmakers.

The second legacy was delivered in person seventeen years later, in 1951. That was the year I visited Rome for the first time. I was sitting at lunch with a woman friend, on the terrace of a restaurant fronting the church of Santa Maria in Trastevere, when two men in clerical dress came out of the church and headed towards the restaurant. The waiter seated them a few tables away from me. One of them was a stranger. The other was Brother Avellino. He was grievously changed. What was left of his hair was almost white, his round face was shrunken and dew-

100

lapped. His hands shook with the tremors of Parkinson's palsy. The dark, shrewd eyes were lustreless and the smile had collapsed into a permanent grimace of distaste for his own condition. Our eyes met. He recognised me. I had no choice but to go to him and offer a greeting. He introduced me to his companion, a man from the Irish province. He invited me to sit down. I declined. My lady was waiting. The man from the Irish province decided he needed to go to the toilet. Avellino said:

'So! It's been a long time. You seem to have done well for yourself. We've all been rather pleased with the fellow we turned out.'

'That's nice to hear – except you didn't turn me out. I chose to go, remember?'

'Sure you did. It was an unfortunate phrase. It was a bold step you took. Have you ever regretted it?'

'Never.'

'I'm glad to know that. I often felt responsible.'

'Why, for God's sake?'

'I played you a dirty trick.'

'I'd forgotten.'

'I'd like to think you'd forgiven me.'

'Forgetting and forgiving go together.'

'Do they now?'

'Believe it, Brother.'

'If you tell me so.'

'I tell you so.'

It was a lie, but I hoped he believed me. In case he didn't, I changed the subject.

'And what have you been doing all these years?'

'Not much. I've always taught junior school. A couple of years ago the council offered me a small Community in the country, with a headmaster to run the school. I was hardly installed when I got this.' He

101

held out his trembling hands. 'There's small relief, but no cure. I resigned. They offered me a trip to Rome as a consolation prize. I took it. Brother Gabriel happened to be here at the same time. He's giving me the grand tour. He knows this place like the back of his hand, which is a hell of a lot steadier than mine.' He hesitated for a long moment and then plunged ahead. 'I've often wished I'd had the courage to move out, as you did, and make another life for myself.'

'Why didn't you?'

He shrugged and flapped his unsteady hands.

'There were always just enough things to keep me going – small gains, small plots, small pleasures, small hopes. The one thing I wanted most of all I couldn't have.'

'What was that?'

'To be a musician. I had the dream in my head, but no ear and no talent, which is why I was always ashamed with you. So I settled for smaller beer. I became – well, an entrepreneur, if you're polite; a parasite on other men's talents, if you want to be brutal about it.'

'I think you're being rather rough on yourself.'

'Maybe I am; I'm in a low state just now. But seeing you today brings up the hard question: whether what I got was worth what I paid for it – freedom, the love of women, children of my own, perhaps. I might have grown into something bigger and better than I am now. If a man's going to lust after the world's prizes he ought to shoot for the big ones, not the penny-a-piece novelties. You should go back to your friend now. She'll be getting impatient. If you still pray, say one for me sometimes.'

We shook hands and parted in silence. It was more of a dismissal than a goodbye. I was not his brother any more. He needed an absolution, but disdained my compassion. He still had the black, stubborn Irish in him. He'd be damned before he'd give me full satisfaction.

That afternoon our stroll took us into the cloisters of Santa Cecilia, the patroness of music. I made the prayer Avellino asked, but it was as much for myself as for him. I had worn him a long time like a burr in my backside. Maybe that's what the haunting was all about. I had always lacked the final grace to forgive him.

He at least had purged himself. I still clung to the most pitiful amulet of all – another man's guilt for my delinquency.

GLUTTONY

6

Rachel Billington
A Time for Tea

When Colette met Harold Gibbon, she was twenty-seven, already older than she liked. But he was over forty, married and made substantial by his formal suit, his neatly-brushed hair. For six months they worked in the same office, an insurance agency where he was agent and she was secretary. Colette was hardly more than five feet tall but made in the shapely mode of an earlier age. She had soft white skin, dark bouffant hair and favoured suits of cherry-red or apricot. She felt herself light up the dark corners of the office and sensed Mr Gibbon felt it too.

One slack Friday afternoon Harold Gibbon looked around the empty room and said, 'How about a cup of tea, dear?'

'You mean outside?' responded Colette, not at all surprised.

Harold supposed he did, although a little amazed at his own daring.

It was geographical accident that they found their way to the Waldorf Hotel, which happened to stand halfway between their office and Charing Cross station where Harold caught his train home.

'Of course my wife seldom comes to London now,' said Harold as they pushed their way along the crowded pavements.

He had not meant to say this, had merely intended to mention his wife as a precautionary measure – he was not a bold man – but the words took command. He frowned anxiously. He need not have worried.

107

'I don't blame her at all,' replied Colette cosily. 'Who would live in London if they didn't have to?'

Actually she loved London, even her part of it in a flat shared with her mother in Camden Town, but it was an engrained rule with her to agree with even the slightest indication of a man's views.

In fact Harold loved London too, its energetic excitement cheering his dull life, and felt he thwarted every day he caught his train back to Sevenoaks. It was at this moment of mutual, misunderstood agreement that he indicated the entrance to the Waldorf.

'We shall have tea here,' he announced with the trace of a flourish.

'Oh, marvellous!' mouthed Colette, glad she was wearing a new jersey two-piece.

Again it was chance that the entrance they had chosen led straight to the Palm Court. They were there at once, ushered in by bowing waiters in dress suits, overcoats removed graciously, and seated at a little table near the dance floor.

'Not too near the band, madam,' commented the waiter, who was elderly and dignified.

Dazzled, Colette could only nod and blush. To step out of the dark, cold and busy streets of London into this large, brightly-lit room where music played, was like stepping into the pages of the romantic novels she favoured.

'Oh, Mr Gibbon!' she breathed. 'How did you find such a place?'

Harold, who had had no plans for such luxury, looked modest and fingered his wallet.

'Please call me Harold,' he thought to say.

'The set tea or a glass of champagne first?' enquired the waiter.

A mood of rare recklessness overtook Harold. Was not this the stuff of his dreams on the suffocating train ride, back to his not very well wife and his not very nice house in Oak View Road? He looked across the table at Colette who was glowing prettily in some soft, red garment and gave her the smile usually reserved for his most important clients.

This is fun, their eyes said to each other, let us enjoy ourselves, for it is all not quite real and in an hour or two life will be back to normal.

'Oh, do look!' Colette's eyes widened charmingly. 'People are dancing.'

Up till then neither of them had taken in the significance of the music, but now several couples had moved on to the shiny wooden floor and were executing well-turned quick-steps.

'Dancing!' exclaimed Harold in a shocked voice.

'I don't expect you like dancing.' Colette modified her enthusiasm, for she loved it, she had even taken lessons a couple of years ago. 'Very few men enjoy dancing.'

But Harold's shock was due to the realisation that fate really did mean to give him a good time, for until the last five or six years when his wife had become not very well they had regularly attended the Sevenoaks Ballroom and South American Dance Club. Harold Gibbon was confident in his quick-quick-slow.

'Shall we?'

Round the floor they went, Colette demure yet yielding, Harold assured yet protective. When they returned to their table it was hard not to let happiness rip. Harold found himself thinking it was lucky there was the weekend between this and their next meeting in the office. Colette did not think but merely existed.

109

'Tea?' she suggested, ready to pour.

'Cucumber sandwiches?' enquired Harold. 'Or would you prefer to start with tea-cakes? Or perhaps even scones, strawberry jam and cream?'

They laughed together. It seemed such a lot to eat, but it turned out that Colette had worked up quite an appetite with all that dancing, and Harold encouraged her.

'My wife, I'm afraid, does not eat much.'

Clearly this was a criticism and Colette, eager to please, ate his scone without too much pressing.

'You have so much life,' commented Harold, and Colette understood that again she was being compared favourably to his wife.

'I am so enjoying myself!' she cried girlishly and envisaged briefly her mother, of whom she was very fond, at this very moment preparing their solid supper of meat and potatoes. 'When we dance I feel as if we're floating.'

Harold was a little wary of this fancifulness and discreetly looked at his watch. Despite the fun they were having, he did not want her to get the wrong idea. At once Colette caught his mood and withdrew a little.

'I mustn't be late or my mother will worry.'

'And I must not miss my train.'

'Oh, no. Your poor wife would worry.'

'Poor Mrs Gibbon,' agreed Harold.

Nobly, Harold paid the very large bill without a wrinkle and they found themselves on their way out via a man-sized potted plant. Colette's rosy lips, sweetened with strawberry jam and a bubble or two of champagne, were irresistible.

'Oh, my dear,' whispered Harold, bending to her, 'you will make some man very happy.'

Then they were out in the cold and the dark and the noise, so that their farewells were brief.

'See you on Monday!' cried Colette, suddenly not caring if this was indelicate. 'And thank you!'

'Thank you,' replied Harold gravely and was gone into the rush of hurrying people.

Colette, who also caught her Underground train from Charing Cross, followed slowly.

This should have been a single, once in a lifetime, occasion of fun. Neither Harold nor Colette had the will to deceive nor did they feel a need to explore their sexual natures. In fact quite the contrary. But it happened the following Friday that they found themselves once more alone and underworked, and at about four o'clock they caught each other's eyes. Colette blushed because she was afraid Harold might have guessed she had bought a new skirt, which was fuller than she usually wore and clasped her waist more tightly.

'I think we should have tea and take some exercise,' said Harold soberly.

'Yes,' Colette was docile. She tried not to smile, just as she had tried not to show her disappointment when he had not mentioned the Palm Court all week.

That second afternoon Harold, as if admitting it was to become a routine, laid down the rules even more clearly. 'I met my wife when I was sixteen,' he explained, 'and she has been the only woman for me ever since.'

Colette made sympathetic noises and daintily ate a fish-paste roll before intimating that her relationship with her mother came before everything. Harold seemed more relaxed after these declarations and when they took to the floor it was his confidence that led them to bring off a flamboyant glide and spin.

111

As before, Colette found herself hungrier than Harold, who admitted, lightly touching his waist-coated chest, that he suffered from his stomach.

'Oh, I have no problems like that!' cried Colette, enjoying his admiration. 'What tiny pots of jam!' she added, showing off further her zest for life.

Their kiss was exchanged once more behind the man-sized plant and they parted as before.

Soon the week could not have existed for either of them without their Friday tea-dance. Even if they could not get away early they made time by discreetly ringing their separate homes, giving late working as an explanation for their delay.

Since the insurance agency was not a big organis-ation Harold and Colette's colleagues soon discovered their secret, but no one was interested enough to do more than snigger behind their backs. They assumed, not without justification, that Mr Gibbon would be incapable of doing anything really exciting.

Yet for Harold and Colette it was just the right level of excitement. Their hearts beat faster, their skin flushed, although Harold's was rather sallow owing to his bad digestion, and they kissed with champagne enthusiasm. No more, however. No further.

They were both amazed when they found they were celebrating a year's anniversary of their first meeting.

'Here's to the Palm Court!' Harold raised his glass. He only took a sip since it was by now established that it suited Colette's constitution better than his. He pushed it over to join the glass she had nearly drained.

Colette, cheeks pink and eyes bright, toasted him back. Carried away, she moved her leg forward until it nudged his. Immediately she felt his withdraw. Quickly she snatched a tea-cake for, to her horror, she found a couple of tears were ready to drop from her eyes. She must not be so childish and spoil everything.

'The teas get better and better!' she cried gaily.

'And so do you.'

Harold took her hand across the table and gave it what she felt was a consoling squeeze. Occasionally he did this behind the potted plant instead of kissing her. Colette always felt a little cheated, although she tried not to mind.

'How is Mrs Gibbon?' she asked now, with only the tiniest edge of malice.

'Not very well, I'm afraid.' He paused. 'When I look at you, your health and vitality I can hardly believe you are both members of the same sex.'

'I am always well,' agreed Colette proudly, which was not quite true. Sometimes she suffered terribly from headaches and cramp. Some weekends just lately she had felt so tired that she would hardly have got out of bed without her mother's goading. But she did feel wonderfully well on Fridays when she was at the Palm Court with Mr Gibbon.

'There's something I must tell you,' Harold leant across the table.

For a moment Colette's heart thudded hysterically but then she knew it would be nothing like that.

'I'm leaving the company in the New Year. Last move before retirement. Lucky to get the chance, really.'

Colette stared at him. Their relationship did not include the right to question.

Harold smiled. Again that reassuring squeeze of

113

the hand. 'But nothing could change our Fridays. I'll have it written into my contract.'

'I see,' responded Colette, not smiling, although it was the nearest Harold had ever got to making a joke. The pain of possible loss had been too great. Through a reassuring bite of scone she heard him continue.

'Yes. My new office is just round the corner. Not far at all.'

In a way, Harold's departure from Colette's working life made their Fridays easier. It had always been a little odd relating to her boss, Mr Gibbon, during the week and transforming him into the gallant escort of Palm Court on Fridays. Now she only saw him in that context and could look forward to the end of the week without the deterrent of his pale working face.

On the other hand it fixed their friendship in an unalterable groove, for now they had nothing in common except the Palm Court and what little information they cared to exchange about their women at home.

Love, about which Colette read and thought a great deal, was never mentioned between them. Harold, it had to be presumed, did not think about it, but Colette was romantic enough to believe, somewhere deep inside himself, he acknowledged they were soulmates. His wife of course made anything more than they had impossible . . . Some women did not have as much.

Colette dug into her second pot of strawberry jam. The waiter brought it now as a matter of course.

'I fear I'm getting quite plump.'

'Nonsense, my dear. Not when you can do the rumba as I just beheld it. Besides, you know how I like something to get hold of.'

Colette smiled demurely. He did get hold of her when they danced, pushing away her hips, swinging her round by the waist, so perhaps it really did not matter that she was putting on weight. Her mother said she ate too much but her mother had become quite bad-tempered lately.

'You shouldn't let me eat your tea,' she pushed back the plate of cakes flirtatiously.

The trouble was she felt so happy with her mouth full of food. Colette had begun eating so much to please Harold and now she did it to please herself. Vaguely she knew it was linked to her relationship with him, because it had started with the Palm Court, but now, as three, four and five years passed, it was spreading through to the rest of her life.

In the evening she lay dozing in front of the television, thinking of Harold and eating chocolate biscuits. In the morning she consoled herself for the long dreary day ahead by popping into the baker's on the way to work. They had profiteroles just like the ones in the Waldorf. They were extra, of course, but Harold never seemed to mind.

As the years passed Colette's shape changed from something approaching a pocket Venus to something approaching a pillow tied in the middle. She was still soft-looking and she still had a waist but only by a considerable effort of will. Yet, basking in Harold's undiminished Friday admiration and relying on her light step on the dance floor, which happily never failed her, she did not cut back. Indeed she wore wide, pleated skirts that swirled round her hips in exuberant celebration and never in disguise.

'You are the best dancing partner in the Palm Court bar none,' averred Harold on their seventh anniversary. 'Waiter! Another cherry tart for my lady.'

They were well known in the hotel. They even rather patronised the waiters, most of whom were after their time. The band too played their favourite tunes and only smiled slightly at the seriousness with which the skinny old man and the plump woman in red took to the floor. It was heart-warming, however, the pleasure they took in each other's company — each week as if they were meeting for the first time.

It was in the ninth year of their meetings that Colette's mother died in the night of a stroke, and between her tears Colette realised that Harold had not kissed her for at least a year. The two things made her very unhappy and after the funeral, which was quiet, she went out and bought herself a large chocolate cake. It came from a French *pâtisserie* and contained so much alcohol that she felt quite tipsy, also sick. She cried some more and was glad it was Wednesday and that she would have time to recover for Friday.

'My mother passed away last Friday night,' she informed Harold.

'Oh, my dear.' He squeezed her puffy little fingers. 'Should you be here . . . ?'

'Oh, yes. She would want me to.' Colette knew her mother disapproved of her teas and dancing with a married man but was far less interested in the truth than concerned that Harold would think her complaining or depressed like his poor wife. To show her gallant cheerfulness, she immediately ate all the sandwiches.

'There is no one like you!' Harold watched her and sighed.

He was thinner than ever, thinner, older, paler, balder. Colette felt sorry for him.

'This eclair is so light, it would do you good.'

Harold rolled his eyes and silently pushed away his plate. 'When you have finished, I suspect it will be time for our waltz.'

Colette had never thought she would miss her mother so much. But somehow her Fridays had seemed to come between her and friends, and now she found herself very much alone. Sometimes she hardly spoke to anyone all weekend. Once the week had started she could look forward to Friday again.

In the eleventh year of their meetings Colette received a message at work that Mr Gibbon would not be able to meet her on Friday. This happened so rarely that Colette was distraught and went half an hour early the following week. She had already eaten the scones by the time Harold arrived.

'My wife is seriously ill,' he said, 'in hospital.'

'Oh, Harold. My dear Harold!' Colette felt blood suffuse her face. In a moment of honesty she acknowledged she wanted Mrs Gibbon to die and Harold to turn to her, not just on Friday but on Saturday, Sunday, Monday, Tuesday, Wednesday and Thursday.

'It is not critical, I'm glad to say,' Harold continued, 'but serious. I expect her out over the weekend.'

Harold was right. Mrs Gibbon lived on, seriously but not critically ill, for the next few years.

Colette grew fatter. Harold grew thinner. Colette became forty and Harold was nearly sixty. Colette's sensual life entirely revolved round food, which preoccupied her to a degree that sometimes terrified her. Yet still when she went to the Palm Court everything seemed to make sense. There, she did not feel greedy and disgusting but the woman who brought Harold Gibbon to life. Still she whirled round the dance floor, even though she could no longer wear a belt, and when women colleagues at work murmured 'Weight Watchers' in her direction she smiled mistily, as if she had a secret, and said, 'I'm happy the way I am,' and here she lowered her voice, 'He is too.' So she was left alone.

Fifteen years after Harold and Colette had first danced at the Palm Court, when a complete redecoration had made the place grander than ever and rather more modern, Colette sat at their usual table, waiting. She had taken to arriving early so that she could have a preliminary glass of champagne and cake before Harold joined her. The waiters co-operated, clearing it away without trace.

But this afternoon Harold was a little early. He stood behind a potted plant – an exotic descendant of the one they used to kiss behind – and watched Colette. She had just finished a sticky cake and was dabbing her mouth and licking her fingers.

Harold was upset. Two days ago Mrs Gibbon had finally died. Although she had been ill for so long, he had never thought she would die. Perhaps, just because she had been ill a long time, it had stopped seeming a threat. He could not imagine how he could live without her. He had hung on, however, to the idea of Fridays. That was something that had never changed, would never change. But now, by the bad luck of arriving early and being in an emotional state, he found himself looking on Colette afresh.

How she had changed! How could he have avoided noticing it before? She was disgusting, like a pink pig with little eyes and snuffling wet mouth. And how could she deck herself up in those ridiculous bright-coloured clothes? They would have been misguided on a woman half her size and half her age.

Harold looked round the room nervously. Since its

118

face-lift, the Palm Court had been attracting a much classier kind of customer. Whatever must they think of Colette! How he longed not to have to cross the great expanse of dance floor and claim her as his own.

Shivering with emotion, Harold clutched the potted plant as if he would never leave its shelter.

Colette, satisfied by her hors-d'oeuvre, looked up now and round the room and soon spotted Harold.

'Here I am, dear!'

She waved cheerfully, as if he did not know where they always sat. But it was her role to encourage. Harold slunk over obediently and slumped down. Even through the champagne, Colette saw something was wrong.

'Harold, my dear?'

'Mrs Gibbon is dead.' His voice was cold, deliberate, informative, his face aimed at the tablecloth.

'Actually dead?' enquired Colette before she could stop herself.

'Two days ago.'

Harold's eyes filled with tears. He had lost his wife and now he realised he had lost his beautiful young dancing partner too. He looked down because he could not bear to see the fat pig, who masqueraded as a woman, opposite him. It was all over. His whole life was over. He would retire and bury himself in Sevenoaks.

'I am so sorry.'

Colette's voice was still light and girlish but Harold could not hear it.

'I just came to tell you.'

He looked up for a moment, not at her but in the direction of the doorway.

'Yes. I understand.'

Colette thought she understood that he must say

119

nothing about the future because it was too soon. A wife was different from a mother. She could see he did not want to dance and was resolved to sit quietly, patiently – even though she longed for a tea-cake. They would be getting cold soon.

'I must go.' Harold stood up, his expression wild. He stared down at the top of Colette's head, which was more bearable for him than the rest of her. 'I just came to say goodbye.'

'Goodbye?' Colette was bewildered. Her hand ached for a tea-cake.

'Everything is different. Everything has changed. I saw it at once.'

Now Colette began to perceive that something was seriously wrong but her longing for the tea-cake had become so intense that it dulled her understanding.

'I must go!' repeated Harold, feeling he had already made himself clear.

'I understand,' repeated Colette, although she did not. However, if he went, she could eat the cake. 'Please, don't worry about me.'

'No. Thank you. Goodbye.'

Taking his chance, Harold fled back across the dance floor. It was not very crowded so he only bumped into a young man doing a trendy shuffle, who commented wittily to his tight-skirted partner, 'Doing the Palais Glide, I suppose.'

Colette did not watch Harold leave since she was too busy eating the warmish tea-cake. It was only after the bliss of satisfaction had subsided that she reviewed his precipitate departure. It was then that his repetition of 'Goodbye' struck her unpleasantly. But it was clearly impossible it should mean precisely that, not after so many years and just when Mrs Gibbon had finally decided to die.

'Waiter!' Colette snapped her plump pretty fingers. 'Another glass of champagne and I'm ready for the profiteroles.'

LUST

7

Michael Carson
Return to Sender

I speak to my son through a mouthful of dry toast. Crumbs drop on to the scrubbed pine table where I rest my elbows.

'I think you should do something practical, son. Don't make my mistake.'

The leather patches on my sports jacket miss the table by an inch or two. They miss every horizontal surface I lean them on – just as what I say to my son somehow misses the point – and the cloth is stretched and thinning. Moira failed for once in her life. Moira, the last wife in this sceptred isle to sit down with her darning and Radio 4 every night, did not put on the leather patches quite right. The jacket should really be put into a display case and kept for posterity. Just as Moira will, if there is any justice, be kept incorruptible in a glass coffin to attract charabancs and miracles.

I speak to my son. Michael spoons home half a Weetabix, his third, and gives me a look. The look, like the patches, misses its target. Too many such looks reach me on every working day, my elbows leaning their thin skin on the teacher's desk. I am as unmoved now as I am then. Meaningful looks all fall short, like blotting-paper bullets oversaturated with ink.

'You can look at me all you want, but you know I'm right,' I say, knowing that I don't know any such thing; knowing that my knowledge maybe shows.

'But I'm good at English, Dad!'

He can do better than that. When did goodness ever have anything to do with it?

'You damned well ought to be, you had me for your teacher!'

'It's the only subject that I'm really passionate about!'

Shall I merely shrug or shall I assume piety? I should do neither, but I do both.

'Beware passion. Passion leads to St Jude's Comprehensive, and St Jude's is, as I believe I have mentioned before on many occasions, a passion-killer. Now you say you're not sure that you want to teach. So don't take English, Michael. It leads you inexorably towards the classroom. English and teaching are as inevitable as Guinness and the call of nature. You're good at Computer Studies too. You may not be passionate about it, but you like it well enough. Can't you live with that? Take that. You can read literature at night to rekindle the passions.'

Yes, that was quite good. A nice homely image inserted on the wing, so to speak, to bring everything down to his level. A newly-qualified Master of Five Pints like my son should get the point.

'An English degree doesn't necessarily mean teaching,' my son says. 'I remember when you were taking me for Careers you often said that employers of every description would be impressed by an English degree.'

I nod. Of course I remember saying such things. I have said a lot of things in class that I do not mean. Every year, for instance, I tell my novice sixth formers that literature holds the key to life. I tell them that and then I give them a reading routine: a play of Shakespeare each week, a dip into poetry every night before retiring to keep the juices flowing. I've said that too. Year after year I've said it. It is time to come clean.

126

'Do you know what I remember from university?' I ask him, man to man.

'No, what?' Michael asks.

He is leaning across to push two pieces of wholemeal bread into the slots of the toaster, his chair on one leg. I postpone the man-to-man temporarily.

'Why can't you stand up and do that like a Christian? You're going to have an accident one day.'

The look again. He is beyond my command. I don't know why I waste my breath.

I sigh, breathe deeply and waste my breath. 'I have forgotten everything I learnt at university except what Dr Griffiths used to say when he watched the couples walking along outside his window, hand in hand. The old bugger,' he was younger than I am now, 'would gaze from the window at the quad and take in all the mini-skirted girls draped around their men.'

'And vice-versa. What did he say?' asks Michael, interrupting as usual.

'Haven't I told you?'

'Maybe, but if you have I've forgotten.'

'He used to shake his head and say, "They think it's love, but it's only lust." I've always remembered that. As for the rest . . .'

'Funny thing to remember.'

'Remarkably funny, I agree.' I nod and laugh into my raised cup, thinking other thoughts which add to the funniness, but not able to communicate them to my son. 'That's why I think it would be better to come away from university with the ability to make computers user-friendly and all that sort of thing. It's what civilisation is all about, isn't it?'

'It was a funny thing to say too,' adds Michael, ignoring what I have said.

127

'It was "power for the coarse". I think it all the time. It's a consoling thought.'

'Why consoling?'

'You'll find out.'

'When?'

'When you get to my age.' We speak together, I realising too late that I have fallen into the trap yet again.

'Did Mum have Dr Griffiths too?'

'Yes,' I reply, wondering if I should be smelling a rat, but enjoying too much the man-to-man feeling to retreat.

'And do you think that is all she remembers from university?'

'No, I do not. And don't you dare tell her what I said.'

No, I don't think that. Not for a minute. I can see her looking at her copy of *Persuasion* as Dr Griffiths made the remark. There was no visible reaction. The Devil's Advocate will not be able to catch Moira there – unless, of course, silence in the face of a tasteless remark is grounds for calling a halt to the process of canonisation. I can also see Jean looking at me and winking, her long legs crossed, the mini-skirt a crimson cincture around her groin – but let us draw a veil over Jean.

'So, what would you say if I said I was determined?'

What will I say?

'I would say that if you are absolutely determined to make a rumpled bed for yourself, if you really only want the comfy chair in the corner of a staff-room to look forward to as the pinnacle of achievement, if you want to be undervalued and pushed into cynicism, then on your own head be it.'

I know what he will reply. I also know what I would

have replied to Dr Griffiths if I had had the guts. I know what I'd tell the old buffer now if I got the chance: *Only lust? It seems like a very precious commodity to me! If they've got it, let them savour it!* Yes, that's what I'd say. No, I wouldn't.

'It doesn't have to be like that. I mean, even if I do decide to teach, I don't have to become cynical.'

'Meaning that I am, I suppose.'

'Meaning that you are painting a cynical picture.'

'You'd have to be strong.'

'You've taught me to be strong.'

'Have I?' Have I?

'Yes, you have.'

His knifeful of butter is poised over his toast, but he looks at me and that beautiful face makes me go weak. *Where did he come from?* Stop it! Let it go! He is right. It need not be the same for him.

'You've always told me that honesty is the best policy.'

I nod. I cannot deny it. My weighty clichés breathed through chalk dust and over the steam that rises from sodden tea-bags.

'I have something to tell you,' he says.

I do not think that I can bear it. The face draws out tears like whacks from a strap, like kids at a crib.

'Don't tell me "I am going to take English at university". I think I already know.'

'No, something else.'

'What?'

God, it must be something serious. He is playing with his food. A bad sign.

'Dad, I'm gay.'

It is now my turn to play with my food. What in thunder does he mean? My son! The son who has brought home girlfriends to disturb my calm on more occasions than I care to think about. Nonsense! What about those pictures I found under his mattress, not to mention the state of the mattress itself. How should I react? Well, I won't rise to it. That's probably what he's after. But I won't.

'Oh, yes?' I ask.

'Yes,' he says, staring at the toast on my plate.

I see that I have crumbled it to powder. Now what? What did I say to Peter Mahon – who was. Poor Peter Mahon! Every boy and member of staff knew about him from the moment his Mum brought him to school at the age of eleven. 'Molly' Mahon, who ran the other way when a rugby ball even hinted that it might be coming in his direction, whose voice failed to break, whose wrists resolutely refused to stay firm, whose prose style was florid, whose tastes were sentimental, who ran messages for rough boys – what did I say to Mahon? 'Have you prayed about it?' That's what I said to Mahon, though we could all see that there was bugger-all point in Mahon praying about it. Mahon was Mahon. Christ had cursed the weeping-willow for weeping and bending over the river, commanded the babbling brook to cease flowing or to return whence it had come.

'Of course I've prayed about it, Dad!'

Did I say that to my son? I must have. That was the wrong thing to say.

'You're having me on.' Worse. Much worse. 'No, don't get up. Don't go, son. I'm sorry. It's just a bit of a shock. I don't know what to say. But what about all those girls? What about Tracey and Sarah and Julie? I caught you in the dark by the shed with Julie, didn't I?'

'That didn't mean anything. I was just trying. I

thought if I tried then I'd change. I've been praying since I was twelve, Dad. I've been confessing my so-called impure thoughts since then too. It hasn't made a bit of difference.'

So-called indeed. Beyond my command.

'What did the priest say?'

'Different things. Do you really want to know?'

I nod. I do actually. It might give me a lead.

'Father McNally said he didn't know anything about it but assured me that if I didn't control my passions my passions would control me.'

Sounds sound. He's said that to me before now.

'And what did you say?'

'A decade of the rosary, I think.'

'Did you ever confide in the Jesuits?'

'Yes. The consensus there was that it was (a) a stage, or (b) my particular cross.'

'And what do you think?'

'I think being gay is just me. It is something I have accepted about myself and I want to give you the chance to know and accept me too.'

Well, I can't. Hard cheese, young man. Not a chance.

'It's a lot to take in.'

'I've tried lots of times to sidle up on the subject, Dad. I'm sorry to have had to put it so baldly, but there really is no other way.'

'Now let me see.' I am leaning on the thin material again, ruminating. 'Gay means homosexual, doesn't it?'

'I suppose so.'

'Tell me how you feel.'

'That's a tough one, Dad. You can only feel how you feel. Still, here goes. The basis of sexual attraction is desire, lust if you like. Well, you are attracted by

131

women: their breasts, their curves, their hair, their – their parts.'

The lad speaks true. Tracey, Sarah and Julie had me seeking out the deaf canon at St Edmund Campion's. All in the heart.

'Well,' my son continues, 'I am turned on by men; by their faces, their muscles, their smell. Everything.'

I stand up, almost upsetting the chair, and flee to the counter. There I look for something to do and push the plug into the backside of the electric kettle. It begins to sigh. I switch off the current. I see my face flesh hanging down, reflected in the mirror surface, Moira-massaged. A tear falls. I switch on the kettle again. I play for time.

'Sorry, Dad,' he says. 'I just want to tell you that I burn, I am on fire.'

I turn and let him see my tears. I want him to know what he is doing to me. Perhaps my weeping will quench the fire.

'It all comes down to what makes you jump,' he says.

I think about that. What wretched piece of Rap gave him that idea?

'But what about love? What about children?'

'What about them?'

'Now who's cynical?' I ask, triumphant. I turn back to the kettle and pull out the plug before the spout can spill steam all over the windows and blot out the view with tears.

'I'm not cynical. I know I'll never be a father to children. That saddens me. But I do hope to be somebody's lover, perhaps a good uncle too.'

'And AIDS? What about that?'

'It's irrelevant.'

'Irrelevant, is it?' I am angry now.

'I do not plan to catch it. I hope that when I fall in love it will be for ever.'

'Or I'll never fall in love!' I sing, though I never could hold a tune.

'I was going to say "Just like Mum and you."'

'Leave your mother out of this!'

He says nothing. I have pulled out my last card. Does he know something I don't? As a teacher I am forbidden under clause 28 of the Education Act to promote the acceptability of homosexuality as a pretended family relationship. He seems quite capable of doing all his own promotion. Bent on pretending. The way the world is it would probably be helpful for me as a teacher to stand up and promote homosexuality constantly. That would be sure to drive the perverse younger generation straight into the arms of good persons of the most extreme opposite gender. Was it ever thus?

'Look, Dad, my homosexuality is a fact. I could easily have not told you; I might have gone about furtively pretending I was straight, and having bits on the side in toilets and parks. Is that what you want? Would that have made you happier? I could even marry, I suppose, but I would be sentencing myself and the woman I married to a life of lies.'

I look at him. A life of lies. I could say something about that. What does he want, the dizziness of lust and the tenderness of love his whole life long? On yer bike. Like the lady in the cuckoo clock shop in Zurich who, when I complimented her on keeping all the clocks at exactly the same time, said: 'It is something that we must do.' It is too. That's about the only thing I remember about that trip to Switzerland. It really is funny what you remember. It is not at all funny what gets forgotten. I turn away, sad.

'No, don't do that! That's what people have been doing to us for too damned long! You must do better than that! Look at me! I am not talking about a choice of lifestyles. St Paul said – on a bad day, perhaps – that it is better to marry than to burn. He wasn't talking to me. No one talks to me, except to try flogging crosses of impossible weight. You're supposed to be the wise ones, yet you offer no practical help or guidance. In your eyes there's no difference morally between the promiscuous gay who flits about from man to man, and the man who tries to stay faithful to one. We're all tarred with the same brush! Do not for one minute think that your reaction will change the fact of my lust. My lust is as strong as yours was and demands expression. By speaking to you about it I am hoping to chasten my desires, to combine them with love. Whether you accept me or not, I shall try. But I need your support, Dad. I can't play Russian roulette. Neither, however, can I stifle what is at my centre. Maybe some of us are swirling round in a cesspit, but it is not of our creation. It is the creation of those who will neither accept nor assist.'

I have to hand it to him. My son can speak. A rare product of St Jude's.

'But you've got one of your own! How can you desire a mirror image?'

He pouts impatiently. Suddenly I see in him the mannerisms of Mahon.

'What are the four sins crying to heaven for vengeance?' I ask him in my teacher's voice. I do not know why I ask him. It is part joke, part last resort.

'The four sins crying to heaven for vengeance are (1) wilful murder; (2) oppression of the poor; (3) depriving labourers of their wages; (4) any combination of the above – even when carried out under the mask of patriotism, our country's good, or supply side economics,' he replies. Then he adds, 'I often wonder what bastard decided to put sodomy with the other three. It isn't fair to mix passion with cold-blooded evil. Where there is passion there is no free will.'

'Well, I don't know what your mother will say, I really don't,' I say.

'I do. Mum knows. I think she's always known.'

I nod. Moira was ever thus.

Moira's bike clicks down the side passage. I frown at the kettle as I put it on. I refill the milk jug and place two mugs beside it. Michael has gone back to the filling in of his UCCA form. I hope. Or has he darted out of the back window to cavort with Julian and Sandy in the woods? Tread on that. At least give him the benefit of something original. We parted mute and subdued, but amicable.

'Many at Mass?' I ask her.

'Six or seven. The Miss Hetheringtons weren't there. That's why I'm late.'

'Everything all right?'

'I think so. Margaret has a cold and Claire decided to stay in with her. They were listening to "Gardeners' Question Time". Margaret says that Claire is mad about Clay Jones. What have you been up to?'

'Michael and I had a heart to heart.'

'Good,' she says, and takes off her coat, leans it over Michael's chair and frowns at a loose button.

I pour the tea and she holds the mug in both hands to warm herself.

'Moira, do you remember Dr Griffiths?'

'Of course. Why?'

'Nothing. Michael told me about his problem.'

135

'Did he? I hoped he would.'

She hoped he would.

'So what are we going to do?'

Moira sips her tea and says nothing.

I repeat the question.

'I think we do nothing. We accept him. God made him. We return the problem to Sender.'

'You admit that it is a problem, then?'

She nods. Then she adds: 'But I think love can solve it.'

'Why?'

'Love's a balm. Michael's heart is in the right place.'

'But his desires aren't.'

'Maybe not.' She reaches over and twirls the loose button on her coat. It comes off. 'Thought so. A good job I noticed it. I'd never have been able to get one that matched.' She smiles at me. 'Why did you ask me about Dr Griffiths?'

'No reason.'

'He was a wise old bird. Jean had quite a crush on him. Did you know that?'

'No, but no one was safe around Jean. Miss Hot-pants the men called her.'

'Well that was the sort of thing you lot would have called her. But you were all wrong about her, you know.'

I just nod. If Moira chooses to be charitable, there is nothing I can do about it, though a wicked part of me is tempted to confess. I have not thought of Jean much in the last twenty years. I have thought about her several times in the last hour.

'She was just a bright, fun-loving girl, except where Dr Griffiths was concerned.'

'I never knew about her and Dr Griffiths.'

'Didn't you? It was odd. Dr Griffiths never recipro-
cated, though he was well known to be a lady's man.
He didn't respond to Jean at all. I always thought she
was the prettiest girl in the place. He once told me
that he preferred the intellectual type.'

That was a funny thing for him to say to Moira.

'That was a funny thing for him to say to you,' I say
after a long pause.

She shrugs, concentrating her attention on the
grain of the table.

I change the subject. 'How long have you known
about Michael?'

'I think I've always known. He's always seemed far
too nice to be normal.'

'What an odd thing to say!'

She reaches for her sewing box under the week's
Guardians on the fourth chair that is always empty.
Then she takes her coat from the back of Michael's
chair and drapes it over her knees. She compares the
colours of thread, selects some, cuts off a length, takes
a needle from a pin-cushion, threads the cotton
through it on the first attempt and sets to work.

'I wonder what's on the radio?' she asks.

'And did you know about me and Jean?' I ask her.

She nods. There is a smile on her lips. 'But I didn't
tell you about Dr Griffiths either.'

What's going on here?

'The Miss Hetheringtons are knitting Clay Jones a
sweater. Did I tell you?'

'No.' What has that got to do with anything?

She answers my unspoken question, as she has a
habit of doing. 'Claire says, "His voice is lovely. He's a
real gentleman." Margaret laughs like a drain, gives
me a dig in the side, and says, "Don't you believe it!
She's beating round the bush! If Clay Jones turned up

137

on his lawn mower and tooted for her to go off with him, she'd be out of that door like a shot!"

I see Moira in her glass coffin, a smile playing on her incorruptible face, charabancs full of pilgrims blocking all approaches to 15 Hope Road. I hoofing it off, sad, to becoming a gardener brother away from the bereft world. Were that to happen would Moira smile down upon me from her high cloud, or would she have flicked through the book of my sin, seen the entries that detailed my off-by-heart adulteries with Jean, with Sharon, Sarah and Julie, with Samantha Fox and Kate Adie, with half the female staff at St Jude's and ninety per cent of the female sixth form? Would that whip her patch of heaven from under her? Would she look at our years together, years of good friendship and once a week lovemaking under the pregnant gaze of St Gerard Majella, as a swizz? I confess. I married but I burnt. Was it better?

'I'm sorry, Moira,' I say.

'Sorry? What about?'

'Oh, everything.'

'You're a good man, Dunstan.' Dunstan is my name, you see. The truth will out.

'No, I'm not. I'm not. If you only knew.'

'I know. Same here.'

'We've forgotten about Michael,' I say.

'No, not really.'

'No.' No.

'Did Dr Griffiths really say that?'

I nod.

'Judgmental little hypocrite!' she says.

That is not like Moira.

'I mean, how the hell did he know what was going on inside those couples? Where does lust end and love begin? Does anybody know? I once read that lust can

138

be like the grain of sand inside the oyster. The sand irritates and the oyster builds the pearl around it to protect itself. The pearl is love. But lust is there. Love just envelopes it.'

'So no lust, no love.' I never itched for Moira. Perhaps our love is a pearl of virgin birth. Stop it.

'You can take a metaphor too far.'

I had not noticed that she has finished sewing on the button. How long has she been knitting? Poland will be a little warmer this winter. I get up and kiss her.

'Time for bed,' I say.

'I'll be up soon.'

I can see light under Michael's door. I dither outside, avoiding the creaks of the landing floorboards. I know the noisy ones as a blind man knows braille. Then I raise my arm to knock at his door, but I do not knock. Of its own accord my hand unfists, and rises to bless the door, and Michael taking lonely decisions behind it. At this moment he may be choosing the wrong subject, the wrong university, making himself the wrong bed to lie in. I do not know, but I like the feeling my blessing sparks in me. I repeat it, thinking of my beloved son in whom I am as pleased as can be.

God's Fool *Julien Green*

An emotionally gripping portrait of St Francis of Assisi. Julien
Green is acclaimed as one of the foremost bilingual authors of
his generation.

'An exceptionally readable and individual work.' *The Guardian*

'Julien Green's book is beautifully written, well-researched,
and altogether a masterpiece. Readers of it have the privilege of
seeming to participate in Francis's sublimely crazy ministry. It
is enchanting.' Malcolm Muggeridge

Searching for God *Cardinal Basil Hume*

Cardinal Hume discusses the problem facing anyone who attempts to obey the twofold command to love both God and neighbour.

'Heartwarming and inspiring – a classic.' *Coventry Evening Telegraph*

'Practical and down-to-earth, concerned not with abstract theories but with daily difficulties.' *The Times*

Forgotten among the Lilies *Ronald Rolheiser*

Ronald Rolheiser comments on our struggle to move 'beyond our obsessions, restlessness, fears and guilts, that rob us of the spirit of our own lives, of the feel of our own cold and warmth, of the taste of our own coffee, and the consolation of God.'

'Ronald Rolheiser invites us to look beyond the surface of our lives. He gives us permission to be human. He is a gifted communicator and I personally value his writings very much.' Delia Smith

The Restless Heart *Ronald Rolheiser*

'Loneliness is not a rare and curious phenomenon. It is at the centre of every person's ordinary experience.' This outstanding book will reassure and free many to life more meaningfully.

'This is not a book to read for an answer to all the problems of loneliness, but for the ability of the author to move us from the danger of the condition to its immense opportunities.' Dr Jack Dominian

'I read this book with a mounting sense of recognition.' Richard Holloway, Bishop of Edinburgh

Also published in Spire:

A Journey into God *Delia Smith*

A profound reflection on a subject of deep personal significance to Delia Smith: prayer.

'A useful and practical guide.' *The Sunday Times*

'A book for the non-believer and, perhaps even more so, for the not-quite-believer – and this must include an awful lot of us.' Barry Norman

'It is like having a wise, practical friend on the same wavelength.' Lional Blue